A GIRL
NAMED
DIGIT

A GIRL NAMED DIGIT

By Annabel Monaghan

Houghton Mifflin
HOUGHTON MIFFLIN HARCOURT
Boston New York 2012

For Gretel Dennis, inspiration and dear friend.

Houghton Mifflin is an imprint of Houghton Mifflin Harcourt
Publishing Company.

www.hmhbooks.com

The text of this book is set in Apollo MT Std.

Library of Congress Cataloging-in-Publication Data
Monaghan, Annabel.
A girl named Digit / by Annabel Monaghan.
p. cm.
Summary: After identifying a terrorist plot, a brilliant seventeen-year-old girl
from Santa Monica, California, gets involved with the young FBI agent who is
trying to ensure her safety.
ISBN 978-0-547-66852-9
[1. Terrorism—Fiction. 2. Kidnapping—Fiction. 3. Interpersonal relations—Fiction. 4. Adventure and adventurers—Fiction.] I. Title.
PZ7.M73649Di 2012
[Fic]—dc23
2011012239

Manufactured in the United States of America
DOC 10 9 8 7 6 5 4 3 2 1
4500355303

MY LIFE IS BASED ON A TRUE STORY

ON THE MORNING OF MY KIDNAPPING, my mom's makeup was perfect. After years of training in television and film, she had mastered how to apply exactly the right amount so that she would appear flawless to the camera, while not looking garish in person. Smoky gray eye shadow framed her lids, and the lightest application of mascara—waterproof for the somber occasion—darkened her lashes. She'd lined her lips in what I knew was her go-to lip liner and filled it in with the palest nude lipstick. To the untrained eye, she looked as if she could have woken up like this, at once tragic and gorgeous.

What surprised me more was her outfit, which had taken some serious thought. Our house is painted French blue, with a darkly stained brown door, surrounded by hot pink bougainvillea that creeps down the walls like ivy. She stood perfectly framed in the doorway in a turquoise T-shirt with the thinnest stripe of the same exact hot pink. Her white linen pants looked crisp against the backdrop and picked up the trim around the door. Perfect. I'm sure I'm the only one who noticed this, as everyone else probably focused on the brigade of television cameras that surrounded her. And the fact that she was sobbing.

One guy from CBS yelled out above the others, "Mrs. Higgins, when did you notice she was gone?" She looked down and whispered, "Gone," and started sobbing again. The hungry reporters realized that, besides the dramatic clip for the evening news promo, they were getting nowhere with her. They turned to my dad, who looked a little disheveled in his normal college professor way, no different at eight a.m. than at eight p.m. Always direct, he spoke right into the camera. "We found the ransom note by the front door at 6:47 this morning. We immediately checked our daughter's room and found her missing. We called the police at 6:55."

A chipper young woman from Fox asked, "Does your daughter have a habit of disappearing? Has she ever been in trouble before? Are any of her friends involved?"

My dad squared his shoulders at the camera. "We have a missing seventeen-year-old girl and a ransom note. The police and her mother and I are treating this like what it is—a kidnapping. My daughter has never been in any danger before this."

NBC local news asked, "Didn't the ransom note say not to call the police? Aren't you worried the kidnappers will see this on TV and harm your daughter?" Dad looked like a deer in headlights. Apparently he hadn't thought this all the way through. The past twenty-four hours had been a blur of constantly changing lies, all strung loosely together. "We have nothing more to say." He and Mom walked back into the house.

I watched this whole scene from a warehouse in downtown Los Angeles on a six-inch TV with an actual antenna. Big-budget kidnapping. Not. I sat on one of two mismatched upholstered armchairs in a windowless room where I couldn't even tell night from day. The only reason I knew it was five o'clock just then, besides the replay of my kidnapping story on the five o'clock news, was that my captor came in with dinner.

He caught the tail end of the segment and watched with me as my mom opened the front door for a second time to offer a despondent wave to the cameras. He plopped down in the other chair and smiled. "What do you want to do now?"

HONK IF YOU LOVE BUMPER STICKERS!!!

OKAY, SO MAYBE I'M NOT REALLY kidnapped. And, okay, maybe this is a little bit fun. And, yeah, maybe my captor, FBI rookie John Bennett, is a little cute in a way-too-old and probably-too-serious kind of way.

I'm not the sort of person who would willingly put herself in the center of the five o'clock news. In fact, I'm not sure that I willingly participated in any of this. The whole thing started with a little math game, and since then I have been along for the ride, running from forces I don't even totally understand. I'm Farrah Higgins. As much as I wish I were kidding, that really is my name. My mom is an actress and devoted the entirety of the 1970s to worshiping and emulating the Charlie's Angels in every way possible. I could have been named for Kate Jackson or even Jaclyn Smith. But, no, Farrah Fawcett was the most famous angel, and when I was born my father made the mistake of saying, "She's a little angel." And Farrah it was. Trust me, I remember to thank them all the time.

We live in L.A., and I know what people say about us: "L.A. is an intellectual black hole, a cultural void. Their creativity is measured by the number of sequels they've produced . . ." And, yes, it bothers me that they think so. My dad's an intellectual, and my mom is, well, less so. But the environment here is teeming with inspiration and genius. Los Angelenos have been known to create things that the rest of the world finds ridiculous, and others that the world can't live without. Either way, people are creating something out of nothing, pulling ideas out of the sky. I love it here.

And, no, I don't even mind the traffic. First of all, the only place I ever drive to is school, so I'm never in such a big hurry to get anywhere. And second, I do some of my best reading in gridlock. I have a secret fascination slash obsession with bumper stickers. I've been known to get off the freeway on the wrong exit just for a chance to finish reading the back of someone's car. I'm baffled that people are just so out there with their thoughts and their identity that they can post their political and religious views on the back of their car for any tailgater to see. And then there's something about the concise nature of the bumper sticker itself, somehow telling you so much about its owner in ten words or less.

I started collecting bumper stickers when I was ten and had my entire bedroom door covered with them by eleven. I'm picky about the ones I put up and use tape for a few weeks before I actually commit to the peel and stick. My four bedroom walls are now completely covered, each sticker carefully X-Actoed around the window frames and electrical outlets. At the time of my kidnapping, I had covered about one-third of my ceiling, but I'll never really be finished. I am constantly covering old stickers with new ones, placing more positive messages over ones that spoke to my preteen angst. It was a good day when ASK ME IF I CARE! gave way to WAG MORE, BARK LESS. For years I've gone to bed gazing up at the eternal question: WHAT IF THE HOKEY POKEY IS WHAT IT'S ALL ABOUT?

I know, I'm a little off topic. But don't dis L.A. — we're on the cutting edge of self-expression. Personally, I drive my dad's old Volvo wagon, and I have nothing on the back. As hard as I try, I haven't come out of the bedroom with my hobby. I'm still looking for the peel-and-stick representation of my Inner Self. Hey, I'm only seventeen.

It's my senior year at Santa Monica High School. I have

a sixteen-year-old brother named Danny and married parents. My mom's a not-quite-famous actress — she always has a job, but she doesn't exactly get mobbed or even recognized at Whole Foods. My dad is head of the math department at UCLA. Yes, that is where all the pocket protectors go to meet other pocket protectors. He's pretty cool, though, and gives me a lot of space to be un-nerdy and to act like a regular teenage girl. He says my gift can wait, but that I only get one chance to be a kid.

Oh, right, so my gift. If you can call it that. There's a fine line between a gift and a disability — "special" can mean very different things, depending on who you're talking about. You could say I'm good at math, but that's not really it. It's like my mind never stops calculating things. Ever since I was a little kid, I've been able to find patterns in things that other people can't see. I can take thousands of pieces of data and arrange them in a logical pattern, or I can take seemingly random data and identify the pattern within it. Like when I was eleven months old, I could put together a 300-piece puzzle, 1,000 pieces by the time I was two. By the time I was nine, I was able to see order in a group of 2,000 numbers. My dad would give me temperature statistics, and I would be able to compare them to humidity predictions and tell him whether it was going to rain. This has very little value really, because you can put numbers like this into a computer and it'll spit out the correlation. The only point is that my mind does this automatically. It was pretty cool until it made me a freak.

In sixth grade I started middle school in a building where the classrooms had the kind of 1960s ceilings that had those big acoustic square tiles with tons of tiny holes in them. If they'd been uniform, I would have been fine. But the rows were uneven, and I was desperate to find order. The first row had 16 holes, then 15, then 16, then 15, then — oh! — 17. Anyway, it was obvious that I was wacked, and it was broadcast to everyone in my class when my teacher suggested that I wear a visor to keep me from looking up during class. I tried it and my grades skyrocketed, my social status . . . not so much.

My gift quickly earned me the nickname Digit, which caught on and stuck. By the middle of sixth grade, my elementary school friends were suddenly busy on the weekends, already sitting at a full table at lunch, and generally distant. Where Farrah had been popular in fifth grade for breezing through math assignments with extra time to help out her friends, Digit was a show-off with an obsessive-compulsive disorder. I managed to make a few friends in my accelerated classes, but not the sort of friends who got invited to parties or even had the confidence to show up at school dances.

The summer before I started high school, we moved to Santa Monica from the Valley to be closer to my dad's work. I was going to start high school with a totally clean slate. The school district was excited to get me for the effect it would have on the state testing scores and, hence, the holy grail: real estate prices. If I could keep the schools looking smart, people would keep paying crazy prices for houses in Santa Monica. Yeah, no pressure. So a few weeks before the start of my freshman year, the administration was clamoring to meet me. My parents headed the whole thing off at the pass by meeting with the principal and various division heads to ask them to be low-key about my abilities. She will outperform on your state tests, they said, but tell no one and try to treat her like a regular kid in class. All of the faculty agreed to the lie: I was never to have a test handed back to me in public, and my performance on school and state exams would never be highlighted or celebrated. No one would ever have to know.

I also started seeing a hypnotherapist who helped me learn to manage my mind. Through (literally) mind-numbing mental exercises, he taught me how to turn my processing center off when I didn't want to use it. The trick was to look away before my mind kicked in and to quickly replace what I'd seen with something easy to process, like a perfect circle or a tree. For some reason, asymmetries and irregularities in nature don't bother me at all. A tree with a missing branch or a tulip with a few missing petals still seems to be in perfect balance. Usually, if a tree is lopsided to the right, the tree on its left will make up the symmetry. It's easy to see the order if you just keep backing up. By the end of the summer, I got pretty good at controlling myself, but I have to admit it was a lot of work. I managed to learn to deal with uneven acoustic tiles, but I could occasionally become completely unhinged if someone sat down in front of me in a randomly patterned madras shirt.

In the spirit of new beginnings, my mom gave me the extreme makeover she'd always wanted to. She insisted I spend the summer growing out my hair and then took me to her salon before Labor Day for a few highlights. Cheryl, who had been putting these exact same highlights in my mom's hair for years, seemed thrilled to see me. "Honey, I never thought a girl like you would set foot in this place. You sit down right here and let Cheryl change your life." I'll admit that the new 'do beat the mousy bob I'd worn since I was six, but I knew better than to hope it was going to change my life.

The wardrobe portion of the makeover didn't go quite as well. Mom spent three days scouring the mall for better jeans, cooler tops, and higher heels. What she didn't understand is that not only is my taste pretty simple, but that I actually can't wear a stripe or a check or, God forbid, a plaid. The fabrics are never precisely even—made in China, not by NASA—and it's too much to ignore for an entire day. The shoes killed my feet, so I always went back to the cowboy boots our housekeeper had left me before eloping to Costa Rica. Her name was Milagros, "miracles" in Spanish, and she had always seemed a bit magical to me. I loved to watch her stomp around our house, vacuuming and dusting in her huge denim dress and cowboy boots. And on her last day of work, she gave the boots to me with a secret smile. I tried them on once a week for three years until they finally fit. I've been wearing them ever since. But I have to say I adapted to the new jeans, because, let's face it, better jeans really are better.

I settled into a comfortable rotation of four pairs of jeans and the exact same T-shirt in six colors, and my mom eventually gave up. "If you want to look like you're in a uniform every day, it's fine with me. I just want you to learn to express yourself." *Maybe we're not all meant to express ourselves,* I wanted to say to her. *Maybe some of us are better off blending in.*

Mom always makes me think of the poster in my middle school guidance counselor's office with the cat dressed in a joker's hat. The caption read BE YOURSELF. (It was right next to the one with a cat desperately clinging to a tree branch: HANG IN THERE!). Great message, almost bumper sticker worthy, but the truth is that it's a lot easier to be yourself in high school if you are five feet seven, 120 pounds, naturally athletic, quick with the funny comments, and good (but not too good) at everything, and if you know where to direct your eyes during a conversation. My mom is that person, and I imagine she was in high school too. She's always herself, but why wouldn't she be?

My goal for ninth grade was to ditch Digit and find a new identity. I wasn't cut out to be Funny Girl, because I'm not funny at all. Sporty Girl was a genetic impossibility, and Slutty Girl? I found out later I don't exactly have the stomach for it. I resolved to blend in, to be a blank slate reflecting the personalities around me without projecting any defining characteristics of my own. It's easier than it sounds. Here's the recipe: I never say anything that would be classified as too smart or too stupid. I never initiate a conversation but respond in a group with "Cool" or "Me too." My favorite song is whatever everyone else seems to be into, and I'm dying to go see whatever movie you suggest. Honestly, it's a pretty easy way to live. All you have to do is shut yourself down and become a mirror for whomever you're talking to. (Also try not to use "whomever," even if it is correct to use it as a pronoun modifying the object of the verb. It qualifies as Digit-speak.) I'd mastered the habit of responding to an assertion with the single interrogative word "Right?" by winter break of my freshman year. And I found myself well liked for the first time since elementary school. Not exactly happy, but well liked still.

That's when I met the Fab Four, the It girls of Samohi. They are, in order of supreme coolness: Veronica (varsity tennis, daughter of Hollywood studio owner, legs that go up to my chin), Kat (varsity tennis, famous for shameless drinking and dancing), Olive (varsity tennis, signed up for the Biology Club in tenth grade by accident because she thought it was sex ed), Tish (varsity tennis, owns exactly twenty-six pairs of black Manolos). They seemed so happy in a deep way, like no one could get to them or take away the confidence that they got from one another. They were surprised to learn that their favorite band was also my favorite band and that I, too, dreamed of someday living on the beach in Santa Barbara. And they liked my boots. Seriously. They thought my boots were epic and that I had this earthy sense of style. I was in.

We've been friends for almost four years now, and it's an odd dynamic between us. The four of them have everything in common: their clothes, the tennis team, an obsession with football stud Drew Bailey. I stick to my uniform, wouldn't be caught dead in a tennis skirt, and can barely keep a straight face when Drew Bailey is speaking. But they like that I join in without making waves, and I like being part of a group. It's almost as if I have a safe place to hide among them, where I blend in and no one sees me at all. It's not perfect, but compared to all the other ways a girl like me can get through high school, it works. Well, it worked until I went and got myself kidnapped.

LIFE'S A BEACH AND THEN YOU DROWN

SO IN EARLY APRIL I WAS hanging out with the Fab Four watching that oh-too-scandalous Tuesday night teen drama when I noticed some numbers in the bottom left corner of the screen, directly across from the network logo in the right corner. These white, almost clear numbers flashed during the first minute of the opening credits of the show. I knew better than to mention it (remember, I'm masquerading as normal), and then the numbers disappeared. I forgot all about it until the next week when a different set of numbers popped up in exactly the same place. I scanned everyone's face to see if they noticed. Nothing. The opening scene started and Jessica's sister was hooking up with her crush, so I moved on.

But the next week a third set of numbers appeared, ever so faintly again, during the opening credits. They were quickly imprinted in my mind, and I felt the process starting. The numbers were lining up with the previous two sets. I was on the verge of slipping into Digit mode right there in front of my friends and in immediate danger of missing the opening scene. I reached into my pocket, pulled out my iPhone, and flipped to the photograph of a perfect oak tree that I keep for emergencies. After about forty-five seconds, I snapped out of it and got back into the show.

But by the time I got home, my willpower was all used up. No tree, no perfect circle, nothing was going to be able to distract me from that number sequence. So I went up to my room and decided to air out that part of me that doesn't care whether I have lip gloss on or whether my thong is low enough to wear with my new jeans. I sat down at my desk and wrote each set of numbers. The first set was 55431. The second was 23185. Week three was 3211911, making the number sequence all together 55431231853211911. I stared at it until order took over the chaos, mostly. It was pretty basic. The first fourteen numbers are the basic Fibonacci numbers but reversed. A Fibonacci sequence is where each number is the sum of the two numbers before it. So start with 1 and then 1, 1, 2, 3, 5, 8, 13, 21, 34, 55 is a classic one. $1 + 1$ is 2, $1 + 2$ is 3, $2 + 3$ is 5, et cetera. So if you take away the 911, it's just a reverse Fibonacci. Reverse Fibonacci 911.

That really got me nowhere, so I got in bed. The Fibonacci sequence was pretty remedial, and the only thing interesting about it was that it was backwards. I started thinking that the Fibonacci thing was just to get us to understand the concept of reversal. And then there was 911. Reverse 9/11? Was this some sort of message to honor the victims of the terror attacks? Was there someone at the TV station who was trying to make a political message about terrorists or foreign policy? Sure, that made sense as long as their most sought-after pundits were teenage girls watching weekly beachside hookups. And, oh by the way, if these girls also happened to be mathletes (a phrase that makes me cringe in its sarcasm) who would be able to decipher the code. Unlikely.

It couldn't be an accident that the code unraveled in a nearly coherent way, but I had no idea what it meant. Surprisingly, I felt pretty relaxed after letting Digit out of the box and giving her a little exercise. I fell sound asleep.

Wednesday morning I woke up with the code on my lips. I walked the perimeter of my room, running my hand along the bumper stickers that covered my walls. I admired my work, the precision with which they were hung corner to corner, almost like bricks stacked to perfection. I stopped at 9/11 NEVER FORGET. I ran my fingers over the numbers, 911. It's the number you call in an emergency, of course. It's a date and a phone number. But why put a reverse in front of it?

With my mind stuck firmly in computer mode, I decided I'd be late for school and just sit down and let it happen. Reverse 911. The numbers flipped in front of my eyes and actually reversed 9/11 to 11/9. November 9. It was now April, so it couldn't be a date for something to happen soon. Did anything big ever happen on November 9? Not in my lifetime that I remembered, so I grabbed my laptop and Googled November 9.

As I read through the results, I got a lot of garbage like movie openings, appellate court hearings, and celebrity birthdays. There were tons of articles about John F. Kennedy. I guess the most interesting thing that ever happened on November 9 was his election as president in 1960. There were pictures of Jackie and him celebrating, and it all seemed so romantic. Her clothes and her gloves and her hair fascinated me. I ended up spending a half-hour poring through these articles. "JFK: The first Catholic President." "JFK: How the Celebrities Loved Him . . ."

Finally, my dad knocked on my door. "Aren't you still enrolled in high school?" he asked, looking at his watch.

"Got distracted," I said, slamming shut my laptop and shoving it in my backpack. I was really late.

"Anything good?" he asked. My dad is always dying to hear about new theories I am developing or codes I am cracking, but he is careful not to make too much of it. I think that until I am eighteen he'd rather see me as a mall rat than a mathematician. But still, he can't help but ask.

"Just a number game in my head. I'm making something out of nothing."

I made it into school by second-period English class. Mr. Schulte doesn't really like me because he thinks I don't apply myself in his class. The problem is that I have English with the Fab Four, so I spend most of the time texting them about how hot Drew Bailey looks today or how gross Tessa Jergen's toes are.

Anyway, halfway into class, Mr. Schulte opened his laptop to look up a quote from a poem he couldn't remember, and his face totally changed as soon as he hit his homepage. No one said anything. Olive, the cleverest of the Fab Four, texted me: *Boyfriend dump him?* I thought, *Well, maybe,* because when he looked up, I saw a tear in his eye.

"Um, kids . . ." he started. "I just saw on the Internet that this morning there was a terrorist attack on a New York airport. A suicide bomber boarded a plane that was awaiting takeoff. Eight people were killed."

Did my heart stop? Maybe. My mind started racing. The numbers, the code — were they revealing a target? I think I already knew, but I had to ask the question: "What airport was it?"

"JFK."

I KEEP PRESSING "ESCAPE" BUT I'M STILL HERE!

THE CLASSROOM ERUPTED INTO A CHORUS of *Oh my God*s. "Oh my God, who could do something like that?" "Oh my God, my grandparents live in New Jersey." "Oh my God, are they coming to L.A. next?" Oh my God. I heard them as if through a tunnel, their voices dissolving into a hum. I knew the details of the bombing were about to unfold, and I knew that I was about to freak out. My body somehow got me out of the classroom, into my car, and then home. I raced to my room and slammed the door like something was chasing me. I had the sneaking suspicion that maybe I was going crazy, that maybe this fake life I'd been trying to live had made my mind bend in a way it could not recover from. And who was I going to tell? "Uh, hello? FBI? Listen just as Kayla was unbuttoning Brendan's shirt in the opening scene of my very favorite show, I noticed some numbers, and, well, I think I know how the terrorists are communicating. Sorry I didn't call earlier . . ."

No, that wasn't going to play. And the whole thing could have been just a coincidence. Although I knew deep down that it wasn't. The more I know about math, order, and chaos, the less I believe in coincidences anymore. Everything I look back on in life that I thought was a coincidence seems now as if it must have been by design. What I really wanted was for someone to tell me my math was wrong.

There was only one person I could talk to, so I got back

in my car and drove a teensy bit too fast to UCLA. I parked illegally in front of one of the fraternity houses and ignored the super-cute shirtless guy sitting on the balcony who was yelling at me to move my car. As I ran, I wondered: *Could that guy be smart? Is it hard to get into UCLA? Maybe he's from out of state? Isn't it really hard to get into UCLA from out of state?* I made a mental note to look into this as soon as I relieved myself of the burden of having to save the free world from the bad guys.

I found my dad in his office, meeting with a bunch of professors. Well by "found" I really mean "burst in on and knocked down two." Aren't you supposed to know not to stand in front of a closed door? Anyway, I helped them up, apologized, and introduced myself all in one breath. My dad looked at me in horror but quickly realized something was up that was more important than this meeting.

"My wife has been training Farrah to make a grand entrance since she was two. She'll be very pleased to hear about this." Polite chuckles all around.

Dad suggested they continue their meeting after lunch, and the professors happily agreed, some of them backing out of the room in a don't-hurt-me sort of way.

"So what have you got?" Dad asked me as he stretched in his chair.

"Terrorists. I saw the code they were sending on TV, and it was obviously a signal that an attack would be at JFK." Dad was not exactly springing into action. "Have you even heard about it? Dad, there was a terror attack." That was the first my dad had heard about the suicide bomber. He was horrified and was certainly paying attention now. He flipped open his laptop and went straight to CNN. Seeing it was so much more intense than hearing about it. The video clip showed Terminal 8 covered in smoke, fire trucks parked in the Arrivals lane where waiting taxis should be. People running from baggage claim empty-handed.

"My God, honey. Seven people. Five passengers and a pilot

and a copilot. Plus the bomber." My dad was shaking a little and sat back down in his desk chair. He took off his glasses and rubbed his eyes. I wondered if he trying to rub the image from his mind or if he was hiding a tear. He went back to the news story. "This is awful. It was a businessman from Connecticut, his wife, and their three children. Could have been so much worse if the bomber had been inside the terminal. It says here the airport's been closed in case there are more attacks. Awful, just awful."

I sat down on the couch opposite his desk. I don't know much about shock, but I imagine this is what it was. The only hope I was hanging on to was that my dad would tell me my math was wrong, that I was overreacting, maybe going a little crazy, and that there was nothing I could have done to prevent the scene I just saw.

"Sweetheart, is this why you are here? Did they let you out of school early because of this attack? Do you want me to take you home? And what does this have to do with a TV show?"

I tried to shake my head clear, walked over to his desk, and wrote down the series of numbers. "Over three weeks I saw these numbers flash at the beginning of a TV show. When you line them up, this is what you get." He looked at them for a long time, and I was starting to get impatient. "Nothing?"

"I see nothing, honey." Dad looked at me with confusion. I met his eyes with a little hope.

"Okay, let me explain it to you; maybe I have this all wrong." Even saying it made me feel lighter. Who did I think I was? Ha! It was probably some copyright information, and I was going to need a few more weeks in hypnotherapy. So I worked through the numbers, reversed them, got to 11/9, and then Googled it for him. I slowed down as I got to the end of my case, the dread in the pit in my stomach returning. I knew I was right.

My dad leaned back in his chair, hands folded on his lap, and smiled that I-love-you-no-matter-how-big-of-a-wack-job-you-are smile I always count on. "I see it, honey, but it's a little far-fetched. I think the truth is that you are stressed out socially and bored academically. Maybe we should work on some college-level stuff at home, not all the time, but just enough to keep your imagination engaged and, well, productive."

"My imagination? I'm not going crazy. Well, okay, maybe I am going crazy, but it's not because I'm bored and need to see codes where they aren't. I'm going crazy because I almost had this figured out at eight a.m., and this happened at ten. Dad, eight people were blown up." I started to cry.

My dad put his arms around me. "Honey, this has nothing to do with you. This happened three thousand miles away to people you were never going to meet. Think about it. Do you really believe that the U.S. government, the FBI, and Homeland Security weren't able to stop this horrible attack, but you could have? It's, well, a little ridiculous, frankly."

I was crushed. He was the only person in my life that I could count on to take me seriously. "Dad, nothing would make me happier than to be hallucinating this whole thing. Maybe spend a few weeks in a straitjacket or covered in Mom's crystals and then just move on. But I have the worst feeling that I'm right."

"This isn't going to end here, is it?"

I shook my head.

"If you want the cable station that is broadcasting that show investigated, it's not going to be by us, so don't get any ideas, Nancy Drew. I'll take you to the FBI or Homeland Security, but I can't force them to take you seriously. This theory is a little thin."

Eighty-five percent of me wanted to believe my dad, wash my hands of this, and watch the tragedy unfold on the news at arm's length. Sometimes I really wish I were only 85 percent me.

DON'T CALL ME INFANTILE, YOU STINKYBUTT POOPHEAD

DAD WAS WORRIED ABOUT MY MENTAL health, with good reason. I think he wanted me to feel like he was on my side but also wanted someone in authority to tell me how ridiculous my theory was. So Thursday morning off we went to the Federal Building to FBI headquarters to line up with the rest of the fruitcakes who have secrets that may be of interest to national security.

We waited in line for about an hour until we were escorted into the Fruitcake Room. I didn't see an actual sign calling it that, but you could tell by the way the people were escorted out in a thanks-for-coming-please-don't-touch-anything-on-your-way-out sort of way that anyone who entered was considered a kook. Trust me, I recognized the look.

We were greeted by a guy, maybe twenty-one years old, in a wrinkled but expensive suit. "Welcome, please have a seat," he said without really looking at us.

"You're with the FBI?" Dad asked, horrified by how young this guy looked.

He met my dad's eye. "Yes, sir. I get that all the time. I was an early matriculate in college and am on an accelerated path in the Bureau. But I assure you that I have adequate training to handle whatever concern you have brought in today."

"Okay . . . I'm Ben Higgins, and this is my daughter, Farrah."

"What have you . . . ?" He looked at me for the first time. "Farrah?"

"Yes," I said.

"That's your name?"

"Yes."

My dad was losing his patience. "It's her name. Can we move on?"

"Okay, sorry. What have you got for us?" he asked, straightening the already-straight papers on his desk.

My dad answered for me, which was annoying but a relief. "My daughter has run across a series of numbers that she believes were broadcast to signal the site of yesterday's terror attack." He laid out the story, wrote down the numbers, and explained what a Fibonacci sequence was in more detail than at all necessary. He can't help himself when he starts talking about this stuff. He spouted out details including but not limited to the fact that Fibonacci was really named Leonardo of Pisa and wrote a book in 1202. He pointed out that Fibonacci sequences are primarily found in nature, in the way leaves are arranged on a stem or in the way branches form on trees. My dad has often told me that he didn't go to a lot of parties in high school. Not much of a mystery there. He moved on to the code that I saw and how I connected it to the attack at JFK. My face got hot as I watched the FBI guy reacting to the story. Was he so stony-faced because he realized we had a clue to a terrorist network? Or was he biting the inside of his cheek, trying not to laugh?

I knew the answer the minute he stood up, put both hands on his desk, and said, "Well, that's a very interesting story. Thank you very much for coming in. And if you get any more messages, please give a call. Here's my card. Goodbye."

My father was annoyed. I mean, he didn't believe it either, but I think he wanted the guy to at least give me props for a good story. "You have to admit that it is strange that those codes can be arranged to give such a clear message. Is there anyone available to at least investigate the station that is broadcasting this show?"

"I know a lot of parents have been upset about the inappropriate nature of that program and . . ." What? Was he like eighty years old now?

"Not the program. The codes," my dad went on. "My daughter believes they're connected to what happened yesterday at JFK . . ."

"Of course. We will look into it. Thank you for coming in." Was I paranoid, or did I see a tiny smile in his eyes as he shuffled us out, official Fruitcakes.

"Well, there you have it." Dad shrugged as he handed me the agent's card.

John Bennett, it read. My future kidnapper.

I THINK, THEREFORE I AM SINGLE

I MISSED SCHOOL THURSDAY BECAUSE OF the trip to the FBI. I missed dinner too because I couldn't bear to make one more trip through the living room, where my parents were glued to the continuing coverage of the attack at JFK. CNN's commentators confirmed eight dead and ran and reran their biographies. The dad was a wealthy hedge fund manager who had battled with cancer as a child. The wife had been heavily involved in UNICEF and was a great swimmer. The children were beautiful and bright and full of potential. The youngest was a six-year-old girl with black curls and big green eyes that promised a future of mischief and fun. The pilot had just reunited with his estranged wife. The copilot had been a competitive bridge player. Footage streamed of burned aircraft parts being tagged and removed from the scene, and the bodies being carried out in bags, as casually as sofas on moving day. I begged them to change the channel, but there was no escaping it. ESPN ran and reran the story of the basketball team that never made it to Dallas for some game because of the airport's closing. The local news examined the safety of LAX and ran interviews with the head of airport security and the local Homeland Security chief. CNBC had the financial impact: the Dow Jones Industrial Average was down 3 percent because of the attack.

My mom led me away from the TV, back upstairs to my room. "Darling, you are going to have to let this go. Just breathe in peaceful energy." She literally breathed it in, eyes closed, and looking like it tasted good. "And breathe out all that negativity, all the violence." Yeah, no thanks. It wasn't quite that simple.

I lay in bed all afternoon and into the night, staring at the ceiling, looking for answers in the words that swam above me. They seemed trivial compared to the tragedy that I could have prevented. What was I doing with my life, hanging out at the mall pretending to shop for stuff I'd never wear? I had always known that I had a gift and had often wished I could return it for store credit. But the truth was that my gift came with a responsibility, and I had completely turned my back on it. I really hated myself at that moment, despised the part of me that wanted to feel safe so badly that I'd disappeared. I stared at the sticker on the ceiling directly above me: "Let him who would move the world, first move himself—Socrates." Great, now Socrates was mocking me.

My body ached with the desire to fall asleep, but I never did. Every time I closed my eyes, I saw the interior of that plane. I tortured myself, imagining the expressions of the waiting passengers at the moment of the explosion. I wondered about the dead and what they had hoped to do when they landed. All I had to do was tune into those codes a little earlier, and the fact was that I hadn't put it together because I'd been too busy hiding from Digit.

I imagined myself on trial. "And how exactly have you been spending your time, Miss Higgins?" Several scenes passed before my eyes. A carefully worded note passed to Veronica in math class, agreeing wholeheartedly that Julia Garcia had gotten fat. A mad dash to cover my early acceptance package to MIT with a dishtowel when Kat stopped by. When exactly was I going to tell people I was moving to Boston?

Or my personal favorite: The night I was supposed to hook up with Drew Bailey. It bears repeating. At the beginning of our sophomore year, the Fab Four heard that Drew Bailey liked me. They rushed over to me, bubbling with the news. I shrugged and maybe shuddered a little just remembering the time I saw him shove four hamburgers in his mouth at once to impress a cheering cafeteria. But then I saw it in their eyes, total envy and admiration. I was going to have to like him too.

So we all went out that Friday night to a huge party where he said he'd be. And as excited as these girls were, the thought of hooking up with Drew was like the time my mom made me try liver and onions. I was going to have to plug my nose, close my eyes, and get it over with. Of course, everything—including liver and idiots—goes down easier with something to wash it down, so I made a beeline for the keg the second we got to the party.

With three sips of beer in me, I stood casually with the girls, careful not to look around or meet his eye. I'd read that trick somewhere—it's in a guy's nature to like to hunt, so you have to make him think he saw you first. I tried to be alluring, a little hair flip, laughing too much at whatever the girls were saying. I repeated my mantra over and over: "Oh my God, me too!"

And, as if by magic, there he was in all of his hunky glory standing next to me. If only we could freeze this moment: He smiled at me with his huge green eyes and wide gorgeous mouth. His tan cheekbones were speckled with exactly eleven freckles, five on one side and six on the other. It was an imbalance I was willing to overlook. I'd seen him before, of course, a thousand times, acting goofy in the lunch line or grabbing some kid's hat in the hall. But I'd never been so close to him that I could fully appreciate how gorgeous he was. And he liked me. At that moment I knew what it felt like to be a regular girl. I knew what it was like to be boy crazy and knew that I'd want to go home and call someone to discuss in detail every aspect of his hair, his shoulders, and his lips. This feeling of teenage nirvana lasted for exactly thirty seconds, because then he spoke.

"Hey." That was his opening line.

I countered with, "Hi." Okay, I'm a beginner.

"I don't see you around the keg that much."

I answered truthfully, "I'm not really a big drinker."

"That's cool. You wanna get high?" I was at a crossroads here. Every cell of my body told me that this guy was an idiot. Except for my lips, which really wanted to see if we could get him to shut up and try again. That getting-high comment could have been a really subtle effort at irony, right?

"No thanks, I'm fine." I was really out of stuff to say.

Tish jumped in to save me. "Did you ever get Little Evan to finish his fourth beer bong?" I assumed she was speaking at some frequency that only he could understand, because he lit up.

"Dude! I forgot!" And he was back in the living room, gathering his friends. He scooped up a passed-out kid who I assumed was Little Evan off of the couch, carried him over his shoulder and out the front door, and deposited him head-down in the garbage can on the curb. He came back inside laughing, high-fiving everyone. I kept my eyes on the pair of sneakers peeking out the top of the garbage can outside, hoping for movement.

Kat actually squealed with delight. "Oh my God, Farrah, you are so lucky."

He strolled back over to us, victorious. I had to ask, "What was that all about?"

"That kid's in my geometry class, and I told him to hand over his report on all those ingenious rocks. He wouldn't, so I told him if I ever saw him out, I'd make him do four beer bongs. He didn't finish, so he got tossed."

Ingenious? I don't think so. "Do you mean geology?" I just couldn't let this go. I wanted to give him every chance to show he had the IQ of someone who had only been partially deprived of air at birth. *Come on, say something normal and show me your teeth again, and this will all be okay.*

Out of nowhere, he busted out with, "Wanna go outside?"

No. "Sure."

He turned and headed for the sliding-glass door. Was I supposed to follow? The Fab Four were staring at me, eyes wide, frantically motioning for me to head outside and claim my prize. They all looked so happy for me; I couldn't reconcile it with the dread I felt.

Kat gave me a little push. "Go!"

I took a deep breath and turned toward the sliding-glass door, just as it was slamming shut behind Drew. "See, he doesn't want me to go out there. Let's just hang out in here for a while."

"Please, Farrah. You're not going out there just because he didn't hold the door for you? This isn't, like, the twenty-first century or something." That was Veronica. I'd long since given up on even responding to stuff like that with her. Was it really my job to explain what century we were in? So, against all of my better judgment and stamping out the last ember of my self-respect, I walked slowly to the glass door and opened it myself.

Drew was sitting on the steps of the deck, again looking like the guy on the cover of a romance novel. His hair was light brown with flecks of blond from a steady diet of surfing and volleyball. His tan arms motioned to me to sit next to him. *Jeez, Farrah. What's not to like?*

I did as I was told and sat down, repeatedly smoothing my jeans over my knees to calm myself. I knew we were here for either conversation or kissing. One I'd done before, the other I had not. But I figured he'd probably been engaged in a lot more lip locks than heated debates, so we were evenly matched. I'd just completed the final alignment of the denim on my legs when he spoke.

"Your hair smells good."

"Thanks. It's shampoo." I was starting to hope we'd both be better at kissing than conversation.

I turned my head to redeem myself, maybe to elaborate on my thoughts about shampoo and the variety of scents there are to choose from, and he swooped in like an eagle grabbing an unsuspecting squirrel with its talons. Except that the eagle approached with something even more horrifying, a giant tongue. I didn't move while he literally pressed his face against mine and shoved his tongue in my mouth. Strangely, it was so much more like eating liver and onions than I'd even imagined. I processed a series of thoughts: *If this is what kissing is supposed to be, then they are doing it all wrong on* The Bachelor; *apparently neither of us is good at conversation or kissing; I think he might have had pesto for lunch.*

That last thought was what really motivated me to pull away and express my distaste for him, the disrespectful way he was treating me, and the whole business of casual hookups. I said, "I feel sick." I stood up, a little shaky from having tasted pesto-flavored liver, and backed up the steps toward the glass doors. As soon as I slid them open, the smell of beer and feet and smoke hit me. Everyone turned to see who was coming in, and just as soon as all eyes were on me, I threw up.

Here's the weirdest part of the story: Drew came in behind me and put his arm around me and my barf-splattered shirt. He shouted to the disgusted crowd: "This girl can PARRRRR-TYYYYYY!" As if a prophet had appeared to explain to them the true meaning of the situation, they all cheered with relief. My head spun as I heard tidbits from the crowd: "She must have hit the beer pong early. Awesome!" Idiots.

And that's how I got the reputation as Party Girl, the beer-drinking, lampshade-wearing lush of my time. For a while I downplayed it but never really denied it to anyone. I mean, I meant to, but I have to admit that I liked the identity it gave me, or just that it gave me any identity at all. I'd transformed into this girl with a dark side and a reputation, and I wasn't sure I wanted to trade it for being the girl who really, really doesn't like pesto. From then on my reputation had a little spike of whiskey to it, no matter that people rarely saw me drink again.

When I finally fell asleep, I was completely disgusted with myself. Was this really my life? I couldn't go so far as to call myself a terrorist, but I was probably an accomplice. I had the information necessary to stop this bombing and just didn't see it in time.

Mr. Schulte called Friday morning to see if I was okay. He assumed I'd known someone traveling at JFK that day. I told him I was okay but just freaked out by the state of the world.

Which really wasn't a lie. How is it possible that some pinhead kid gets to sit behind a desk and decide whose information was useful to save people's lives? If it was going to be Bennett vs. the Bombers, I wasn't sure I wanted to watch the rest of the game.

WHEN EVERYTHING'S COMING YOUR WAY, YOU'RE IN THE WRONG LANE

I IMPRESSED MYSELF BY MAKING IT downstairs for breakfast on Friday. I really had no appetite, so I sat and stared at my juice for a while, carefully adjusting the glass so it was in the exact center of my plate.

Danny walked in, drank my juice in one gulp, and sat down. "What's wrong with you now?" he asked me. The funny thing about Danny is that there is never anything wrong with him. He exists with such ease that it is almost an art form. He moves easily in and out of any group, making friends and cracking jokes like he's sprinkling pixie dust around. It's that easy. He can take up any sport or pop into any club and is usually fully embraced. Though he doesn't really care if he isn't. If his magic didn't work equally well on me, I'd probably hate his guts.

On the downside, he has the unbelievably annoying habit of playing the ukulele at all hours of the day and night. I've advised him more than once that girls like guys who play the guitar but probably fear guys who play the ukulele. His response is always the same, like he doesn't get what I'm trying to tell him: "But I like to play the ukulele." So that's what he does. I don't know why I bother—he is the last person in the world who needs my advice.

On this particular morning, I had no patience for his company. "I'm fine. Just realizing what a total waste I am."

He got up and shoved three pancakes in his mouth. "I could have told you that, Digit. See ya." And off he went. No brains, no headaches.

I screwed around all morning on Friday, making myself crazy by reading everything on the Internet about the attack. I tried to find a link between terrorists and beach hookups. Nothing there but sand. Finally I went to the show's website. I followed about a thousand links to the local station that carries it and got myself an address. What else could I do? My head pounded, my heart ached, and I really wanted to sleep that night. I needed to know what was up.

I sent my mom a text lying that I was feeling better and going to school. I raced to my car, hoping I could move fast enough to avoid changing my mind. I drove to Anaheim in heavy traffic, following a Buick Sedan that said: I'M NOT SUFFERING FROM INSANITY — I'M ENJOYING EVERY MINUTE OF IT! Lucky guy. It took me an hour and a half to get to the Anaheim exit, but the address for the television studio was only minutes away. I pulled into the partially underground parking garage, barely comforted by the bits of natural light that came in through the concrete windows. I sat in my car for a few minutes, tired and hungry: What the hell was I doing there? Any normal person would have backed up and gone home. But I knew that if I ever wanted to sleep well again, I had to go in there and find out what was going on. Looking back, I think I secretly hoped that whatever I found in there would be completely innocuous, that they'd describe a puzzle contest the station was running. Maybe I'd won, and the prize was a total absolution of my conscience and an iTunes gift card. Wouldn't that be nice? I went inside.

The lady at the reception desk adjusted her wig a little too far to the left. "May I help you, dear?"

"Yes. I am here about your Tuesday night programming."

A well-dressed guy in his thirties came out into the reception area and started flipping through the in-box. He had black curly hair and a serious unibrow.

"Yes, dear, I know the show that all you girls like," she said.

"Well, I was wondering, is this the station that broadcasts it all over the country or just locally?" I was trying unsuccessfully to sound casual.

The man looked up. "We broadcast in seventeen markets around the country."

My nervousness quickly progressed from profuse sweating to diarrhea of the mouth. "Oh, okay. So you put up the station identification logo at the bottom right corner and, um, everything else on the screen, like the other numbers and stuff?"

His eyes narrowed and he took the tiniest step closer to me. "What did you say?"

Abort! I realized at that moment that I had gone totally mad. I was standing here in Anaheim on a wild hunch, chasing a theory that even my math-obsessed dad didn't like. Best-case scenario: We'd forget about this. Worst case: I was standing in front of a terrorist and had just shown my hand.

"Oh my God," I said in my best Fab Four voice. "I, like, love that show and was wondering if you were going to continue for another season because my friends and I are going to have, like, a huge party at the end of this season, and we really want to have something to, like, look forward to in the fall?"

"We don't decide if the show stays on," he said, stepping closer still, eyes intense as if he were memorizing my face.

"Okay, then, thanks!" I backed into the door before I actually turned and got through it, then ran all the way down the stairs to the parking garage to my car. I got in, locked the doors, backed into a Dumpster, and raced out of there.

I turned up the radio and started to laugh. Maybe I needed to try harder to fit in and really keep Digit in the closet. Maybe I should just go full force and make Drew Bailey my boyfriend and stay drunk until graduation. Maybe I should start wearing black eyeliner and get really skinny. Or maybe . . . maybe that car is following me way too closely.

I looked in the rearview mirror and saw him. The creepy guy from the station in a white Chevrolet. *He knows I know,* I thought, *and I'm history.* My fight-or-flight instinct kicked in big-time and so did my accelerator. I didn't really have a plan but was hoping something was going to appear to guide me. Maybe a big sign saying: "Safe haven, stop here, no bad guys allowed." Maybe a police station? That was the best thing I could think of, but the only police station I knew of was in Beverly Hills. I saw the entrance to the 405 freeway and got on, heading north.

Creepy was right on my tail. I accelerated as well as I could in my 1988 Volvo wagon. You can say a lot about the Swedes and their great love of safety. But speed? Not so much. I eventually got up to sixty-five mph, and Creepy had no trouble staying right with me.

When the exit for Wilshire Boulevard came into sight, I started talking out loud, like I was the GPS lady. "Farrah, take this exit, you will drive two miles down Wilshire and make a left on Cañon Drive just after you pass Tiffany's. You will make a left on Santa Monica Boulevard. You will be fine."

I took the Wilshire Boulevard exit, driving way too fast to have time to think when the exit split into a choice of two smaller ramps: Wilshire West or Wilshire East? In three seconds I had these thoughts: Is Beverly Hills east or west? West is toward the water, and the Westside is considered the fancy part of town; Beverly Hills = fancy, therefore it must be west. Well, give the little lady a lovely parting gift (and maybe a break since I've only been driving for a year) because that answer is INCORRECT.

I found myself driving west on Wilshire Boulevard, away from the Beverly Hills Police Department and the only safe place I knew. Creepy was now in the lane to the right of me, giving me a closed-mouth smile like he knew I'd just made the biggest mistake of my life. There were gravestones behind him, and I took that to be a bad omen. But then I remembered that the VA graveyard was across from the Federal

Building and looked left to see the building looming in all of its windowless grandeur. A crowd of protesters paced outside with signs expressing outrage over lenient car emissions laws: CHANGE THE LEADERS, KEEP THE CLIMATE. Finally, some good guys. Did it make sense to stop here and give the FBI another chance? I didn't see what other choice I had.

I ran a light and made a left-hand turn into the Federal Building's parking garage. I was fully prepared to run down anything in my path until I saw the security checkpoint, complete with three Vin Diesel look-alikes and a metal arm that would have made my Volvo the first convertible of its kind. I skidded to a stop and turned around to see Creepy's car stopped behind me. The security guys were coming to the driver's side of my car. They'd never believe me and let me in. I'd be shot before I had a chance to explain. Now Creepy was getting out of his car too. I took off my seat belt, made a break for the passenger door, jumped out, and ran toward what I hoped would be the safety of a crowd of protesters.

They were packed into the allotted protesting spot, a long patch of grass that runs the length of the Federal Building, separating it from Wilshire Boulevard. They teetered precariously between being arrested for blocking access to the building on one side and falling off the curb into traffic on the other. They moved as a single unit, swaying with their signs of protest in nearly the same rhythm as the palm trees behind them. I bolted through the crowd's membrane and entered another, louder dimension. I wedged myself between a huge man in a polar bear suit and an arguably larger woman. I craned my neck to read the polar bear's sign: HOT ENOUGH FOR YA? The crowd shouted, "One Earth, One Chance, One Earth, One Chance!"

My drably colored clothes and my not-quite-average height were all I had going for me at this point. I scanned the crowd for Creepy until I saw his dark suit move through a gap between the swaying bodies. He teetered with the crowd, edging perilously—I hoped—close to Wilshire Boulevard. I nosed my face into the furry back of the polar bear and tried to figure out what to do next. Soon the crowd would disperse to go have a few drinks and mourn the ozone layer. I'd have nowhere to hide. I saw his suit struggling to move closer. It was being pushed left and right, up and down, to the rhythm of "One Earth, One Chance, One Earth, One Chance!" I knew how disoriented he must be, but in a minute he'd adapt. I gave my polar bear one last squeeze, took a deep breath, and sprinted from the back of the crowd into the garage of the Federal Building.

I can't say for sure why I thought I'd be safe trapped in a dark parking garage, but I knew that they wouldn't let Creepy in there and that my best chance of survival was to be arrested. I had to make sure I'd broken enough rules that the security guys wouldn't just send me on my merry way.

With this idea at the core of my half-baked plan, I ran through the parking garage looking for something to smash or someone to kick in the shins. Any infraction would get me arrested for sure; wasn't I already trespassing and evading security? To make sure, I did the following (for real): I started jumping up and down and making huge circles with my arms, cheerleader style. They saw me all right. It seemed I'd done enough to get cuffed and perp-marched into the building. Thank God.

99% OF BEING SMART IS KNOWING
WHAT YOU'RE DUMB AT

TWO OF THE SECURITY GUYS LOST interest by the time we got into the garage entrance to the building. At five feet four and 115 pounds, I probably didn't seem like a big flight risk. The remaining security guy put his index finger into the print reader for admittance, while never letting go of my left arm. Overkill, right? Where was I going to go with my arms cuffed behind me?

"Where are you taking me?" My heart was still racing from the chase.

"Intruder interrogation."

When we got to the lobby, I immediately recognized the line of kooks waiting to report conspiracies. I knew just how they felt. I was led, cuffed, along this line, drawing the sympathy of everyone in line until I arrived at the front. It seemed I'd cut the line to the Fruitcake Room.

John Bennett sat behind his desk, nodding into the phone. "Yes, I'll handle it. She sounds harmless, but I'll exercise caution and . . . Okay, bye." He put the phone down and started talking before he looked up. "Do you have any idea how serious an offense it is to . . ." He looked up and recognized me. A half smile crept onto his face. "You were here with your dad, Mr. Fawcett, was it?"

If I had a dime for every time I heard that one. "No, it's Higgins. I'm Farrah Higgins."

"Right, right. With the flashing-numbers conspiracy code. I remember now."

Was I being mocked? To my face? Was that a slight smile or a slight smirk creeping up on the side of his mouth? The security guard uncuffed me, and I plopped down in the less than hospitable metal folding chair that he offered—Fruitcake Hot Seat. I took a deep breath and tried to compose myself enough to tell my story. But, against all of my better judgment and in spite of my desire to seem sane, I dropped my head into my hands and burst into tears. I couldn't get it together. I hadn't slept in three days, I was just in a high-speed chase (as high speed as L.A. traffic would allow, but still), someone wanted to kill me, and no one believed me. This went on for a few minutes. Nose running, the whole thing.

John Bennett got up and came to sit next to me in the other metal chair, hankie in hand. What guy outside of a Jane Austen novel keeps a real linen hankie in his pocket to offer to hysterical women?

"My mom always insisted. It's sort of a habit." Apparently, I'd said that last bit out loud.

"Thanks." I took the hankie and wiped my eyes and nose. Here's a situation that may be as outdated as the hankie itself: What do you do with the snotty hankie once you're done? You have to give it back, but it's disgusting. Do you hand him the hankie and risk smearing your boogers on him, or do you shove it in your pocket and promise to return it in a tiny little dry-cleaning bag?

"It's okay; just put it on my desk." Help! My internal dialogue had completely failed me! Why was I saying all this crazy stuff out loud? Deep breath.

"Listen, do you want to tell me why you broke into our parking garage? How old are you? Are you in high school?"

I felt about twelve. "I'm a senior at Samohi. I'm seventeen, almost eighteen. In June." Usually when people are telling you they are almost something, it's more like "I'm almost six and a half."

"So you're seventeen. Is this all about the secret flashing terror codes?" Mocking me again. Good, because I think more clearly when I'm pissed.

"Yes." I just wanted to get up and leave. But I didn't know who was going to be waiting for me when I got back to my car. Plus, I think I might have been under arrest or something. "And if you want me to explain why the codes were such an obvious message about the attack on JFK, I can do that."

"I'm listening." He leaned back in the metal chair and folded his arms in a this-ought-to-be-good sort of way.

I was hoping he'd just take my word for it. I wasn't really in my comfort zone, and I couldn't remember the last time I'd talked about numbers with anyone but my dad. Talking about them with normal people always ended up being a little isolating. It's as if they hear me out and then slowly back away, like I was holding a gun instead of a pencil. I just wasn't in the mood to have that experience with this guy who already thought I was a freak.

"There are a whole lot of people out there waiting to regale me with conspiracies. And you are potentially in a whole lot of trouble. So I'd take the chance to explain it, if you can."

If I can? That got me going. "All right. The network broadcast three sets of numbers over three Tuesday nights. They were 55431, then 23185, then 3211911, making the number sequence all together 55431231853211911." I looked up at him to see how glazed over he was. He was still listening, dark eyes focused and eyebrows furrowed a bit.

"How do you even remember all those numbers?"

"I have a thing for math. Want me to write this down?" He slid me a sheet of paper and handed me a pen from his jacket pocket. It was inscribed PRINCETON ALUMNI. Not bad. I started writing the numbers by memory. "Got it?"

"I guess. So what?"

"So let's separate out the last three numbers, 911. And then let's reverse the remaining first fourteen numbers: 1, 1, 2, 3, 5, 8, 13, 21, 34, 55. Anything?"

"Is this the Liberace thing? I wasn't really . . ."

" . . . paying attention? I could tell. It's Fibonacci. In a Fibonacci sequence, each number is the sum of the two numbers before it: 1 + 1 is 2, 1 + 2 is 3, 2 + 3 is 5. So it's a reverse Fibonacci sequence, followed by 911. At first I thought it had something to do with 9/11, but it's so deliberately a reverse that I looked into 11/9, which happens to be the day that JFK was elected. A long shot, right? But then JFK was bombed the next day." I looked up, braced for John's reaction.

He was looking at me, working the half smile. There was no mockery on his face, just sort of admiration and enjoyment. It was a little the way my dad looks at me at moments of mathematical revelation but different somehow. "So you're a genius." It wasn't a question. "Named Farrah."

"Something like that." I felt a little empowered by the recognition. What did I care what he thought, anyway? "I have a gift for math and patterns and puzzles. I had a perfect score on the math SAT, the math subject test, and the AP Calculus exam, and I had the highest score in the country on the National Gifted Math Students Exam. I'm going to MIT in the fall." There. I said it. And it hung in the air for too long for my liking, so I went on. "After you were of so little help on Thursday, I decided that I needed to investigate myself. I went to KPOP, the local station that broadcasts the show, to see what I could find out. I went all the way to Anaheim and found out very little except that the guy who presumably runs the station is incredibly creepy. I guess I asked too many questions when I was there because when I left he chased me all the way here. Which could not be a coincidence."

"In his car?"

No, on a secret terrorist witch's broom. "Yes, in a 2007 Chevy Impala, white." And your shoulders look really good in that crisp white shirt. I checked his face for shock. Nothing. My internal monologue seemed to be cooperating again. "You can see him on the security tapes from the parking garage. You do have security cameras, right?"

He smiled, both sides of his mouth up now. Was this guy too old to be cute? I mean cute in a nerdy-wasn't-cute-at-the-beginning-of-the-movie-but-was-super-hot-by-the-end sort of way? Maybe it was just the fact that he was listening to me. All patience, he said, "Okay. Let's go check out the security tapes and see if we can identify your broadcast bomber."

The mocking was back, but it felt like progress. John escorted me out of his office. I say "escorted" because it is rare that a man opens the door and guides you gently by the elbow to where he wants you to go—I'd gone into the FBI and stumbled upon Mr. Darcy. We walked down a long hall into the security room. It was no bigger than a walk-in closet with twelve televisions on the long wall and a guy who looked like he stared at screens for a living.

"Ken, may we have the parking garage security tape for the hour ending 1300 hours?"

"Sure, you want to watch that crazy hottie running wild past security? I love it, thinking I'd put it on YouTube if it wouldn't get me fired." Apparently he did not see me standing behind John.

John laughed and stepped aside, with a dramatic wave of his arm. "Ken, I'd like you to meet Crazy Hottie, of security film fame."

I waved, eyes down. We took the tape and went back to his office to watch it. I guess the good news is that not much happens in the parking garage of the Federal Building. It didn't take much fast-forwarding to come across my performance.

John smiled and shook his head. "What were you trying to do?"

"I was trying to get arrested, okay? Now rewind to before I got into the garage. You have to see the guy behind me. That's him. Zoom in on his face—can you do that?"

"Yes, I can do that," he said patiently. "There he is. You're right—he does look creepy."

"Right? Is he a known terrorist? Is he on the Most Wanted list?"

"I have no clue who he is."

"Are you kidding me? Don't you have a database of photographs of known operatives in the L.A. area? Can't you scan his face and come up with a match?"

"*CSI* fan?"

"Never miss it. Miami and Vegas."

I had a feeling that either John had nothing else to do (which was unlikely given the length of the Fruitcake Line outside his door), or he thought this was a fun diversion.

We printed out Creepy's face and went up three flights to what passed for their CSI lab. It differed from TV in two major ways: first, it was populated by both attractive *and* unattractive people and, second, the lights were on. All the way.

John took our photo and scanned it into one of the workstations, typed some stuff in, and said, "Now we wait. This could take a while. Our system has over one million . . ." *Beep.* A match.

And there it was—a profile shot of Creepy, right next to the parking garage shot.

"Jonas Furnis." John was staring, stunned, at the screen. "Time to call my boss."

GOT ISSUES?

JOHN PULLED OUT HIS PHONE TO arrange for someone to cover the Fruitcake Room. Then he called his boss and asked if he could meet with him urgently.

Now this was the attention I'd been waiting for. He definitely believed me, and I was definitely thrown a little off-kilter by it. We took a third elevator bank, more fingerprint reading, to get to the boss's office.

Steven Bonning was sitting behind his desk, banging furiously on his computer keyboard. His desk was covered with precariously stacked paper, coffee cups, and a half-eaten hot dog. He looked about fifty and in need of a comb. "What is it, John?" The fact that a teenage girl was also standing there did not seem to register.

"Steven, this is Farrah Higgins. She seems to have discovered a terror cell working in L.A. that may have been responsible for the events at JFK this week. They appear to be connected to Jonas Furnis."

I straightened a little, waiting for the confetti to start falling from the ceiling. "Well, it was nothing. I mean, I was glad I could . . ."

John jumped in and recounted in his robot's voice the events of the past few days, starting with the code on my TV and ending with the Creepy match. John and his boss looked at each other meaningfully and did not say a word.

Steven stayed seated behind his desk; in fact, he hadn't

really moved since John started talking. He looked very calm except for a single bead of sweat that dripped down the left side of his face.

Silence is so awkward, isn't it? I jumped in. "So you guys have his picture and his name, you even know where he works, so I guess you should go arrest him, then? This Jonas guy, I mean."

Steven smiled a little sadly at my naiveté. "It doesn't really work like that. He would be aware of being identified. He is gone by now; family moved away by the morning; TV operation wiped clean of anything incriminating." He spoke slowly and punctuated each sentence with the strangest tic: after each phrase he shook his shoulders twice in a way that seemed almost involuntary and then punched his left fist into his right. Shudder, shudder, punch. I'm no expert, but it seemed like this guy could benefit from some hypno-relaxation techniques.

John added, "And this guy isn't Jonas Furnis himself. He's a known terror operative working within the Jonas Furnis organization."

"What's Jonas Furnis?" I asked, though I had a feeling I really didn't want to know.

John answered. "Jonas Furnis himself has not been spotted in over seven years and is presumed to be dead. He's the son of groundbreaking environmentalists who did a lot of work in the mountains of Colorado in the early eighties. They both died of cancer in their fifties, leaving Jonas Furnis alone and committed to waging war against the environmental toxins that he believed were responsible for their deaths. He was in and out of jail for arson at several small manufacturing plants that didn't meet EPA standards during the mid-nineties. Those arrests won him a huge following, which has grown and evolved into a major eco-terror organization. Over the past ten years, they have moved into torturing and murdering individuals who they felt were 'enemies of the natural world.'"

"Then why attack an airport?"

"I don't know. Maybe as a protest over how much oil we use?"

Steven was shaking his head, eyes closed. "No, the event at JFK was targeted. They hit a new jumbo jet flying out of that terminal. It was a full-size private jet that accommodated only five passengers in extreme luxury." Shudder, shudder, punch.

"The least green way you could possibly travel." I'm not shy about stating the obvious.

John sat down in the chair opposite Steven's desk and motioned me to the one next to it, stony-faced again. Whatever this Jonas Furnis thing was really brought out the darkness in him. Was this the same guy who was busting on my secret codes twenty minutes ago? "Farrah, these guys have a huge, nearly untraceable network. Until now their terror attacks have been on a smaller scale, just a few individuals. But if they were responsible for Wednesday's attack, then they are getting bolder and more organized, and they are more dangerous than ever."

Why did I feel like he was making this my problem? "But can't you just track down that one guy who was after me and at least end my connection to this whole thing?"

John shook his head. "Jonas Furnis's operatives are everywhere. They operate all over the world and represent forty-three nationalities that we know of. The only thing they have in common is that they are willing to kill or die to protect the environment. And this guy—we know his name, but he's vanished by now. The problem is that you have not. They know you can identify him. They know what kind of car you drive, they have your license plate number, and they likely have your address. You are not safe. At all."

Steven got up and started pacing the length of his desk. "You're sure it's them? I agree it can't be a fluke, I mean, if he followed her and is a known operative for Jonas Furnis. And the Fibonacci thing. God, they love their Fibonacci. They call it the code born of nature—you know, the pineapple, the pinecone, flower petals, or whatever." He ran his right hand through his silver hair repeatedly, adding the finger comb to the beginning of a series of shudder, shudder, punches. "They are going to come after her. They know . . . I can't keep them from kidnapping . . ."

Wait. What? "Kidnapping?!" I wanted to shake him.

John became strangely calm in the face of his boss's flipping out. There was no levity left to him, no smile, half or otherwise. "Kidnapping is their specialty. Kidnapping and torture, really." He turned away from Steven, now collapsed in his desk chair with his head in his hands.

I noticed for the first time that the fist he'd been making with his left hand was not a fist at all. It was just a fingerless palm, perfectly square. I tried not to stare, but sometimes staring has a mind of its own.

John lowered his voice as if he didn't want to upset Steven further with the details. "Jonas Furnis is well known for their kidnapping tactics. If they want someone, they will find them and take them, no matter how they are protected. Sometimes the kidnappings are ideologically motivated, but sometimes they're more strategic to protect the organization from exposure. Like in your case."

Uh, freaking out here. "What do they do with you once they have you?"

"They torture you and brainwash you. Or they kill you. No one, well almost no one" — he turned away from Steven even farther — "comes back as they were."

"I really don't want to know. But, Farrah, how old are you?" Steven asked.

"Seventeen. Eighteen in June." There I go again.

"Oh Jesus." Shudder, shudder, punch.

I LOVE MY COUNTRY. IT'S THE GOVERNMENT I'M AFRAID OF.

ᴄ

BY DINNERTIME—AND, YES, I was starving—my parents arrived and were fully debriefed. Dad was somber and seriously concerned for my safety, but there was a flicker behind his eye that told me that he was delighted. Over the past few years, it had been painful for him to watch me hide out. As much as he wanted me to have a fun and normal life, I wondered if he felt the strain of the charade as much as I had. My gift is much like his and has always been a serious source of bonding between us. I always suspected that he felt like he'd lost me during those years that I pretended it didn't exist. At this moment I could tell he was proud that I had been right, and he was proud that I was being taken seriously by the freakin' FBI. Mom, not so much.

"So, you're telling me there's an organization of terrorists out there who now wants to off my daughter for having added up some numbers on the television?" She was incredulous.

"She broke their code, yes. But they could easily make up another one. And they can find another way of disseminating their messages. It's more that Farrah can positively identify this guy. He must be higher up in the organization than we believe if he wasn't told to just slam his car into hers, killing them both. They must need him for something . . ." John clued in to the fact that he was freaking my parents out. "We may never know what. But we are prepared to protect Farrah at all costs." Nice save.

"You are going to rip Farrah out of school at the end of her senior year so that she can live holed up in some FBI hideout . . . My God! It's only two weeks till the prom!"

John jumped in. "The agent assigned to the case will have the support of the entire Terrorist Task Force to keep Farrah safe, but they will be more or less camping out until this is over. We are convinced that your daughter is in extreme danger and that she needs to be hidden until this terror ring is disbanded and, well, we think her gifts would be of great use to us in making that happen."

Shoulders back. I'm da man. Dad caught my eye and winked at me.

"Can't you at least put her up in a hotel while she's hiding? The Peninsula has a great reputation for service, and the spa is . . ."

John cut her off and managed to stay completely professional. "The terror cell in question has very little regard for the safety of innocent bystanders. Putting a target in a hotel would be endangering everyone in the vicinity. We must keep her in a remote, secure, and substantially less luxurious location."

Steven jumped in with, "And we are going to have to do more than hide her. If Farrah vanishes, they will know that we have her and they will come after you for leverage."

Mom had had enough. "So, how do you suggest we hide her and protect ourselves at the same time? Do we all go into hiding? This is ridiculous."

"No, Mrs. Higgins, we have to fake a kidnapping. They'll think one of their own people took her. It might buy us enough time to find them."

John immediately picked up on the plan, like this was something they did all the time. "Jonas Furnis is very careful about direct communication within the organization, as they know that the FBI and every major government are tracking them. They generally operate by communicating with high-level spies that they have placed in key government jobs and then use that person as a central hub of information. Even that communication is coded to an absurd degree. Our hope is that their communications are convoluted enough that they won't figure out that none of them has kidnapped Farrah before we can find them. We will send police and press to your house in the morning. We will send an agent to spend the night with you in case there is any activity before then. Unfortunately, there won't be time to get Farrah a change of clothes before we go into hiding . . ."

"That won't be a problem," Mom said, rolling her eyes at me and my uniform.

"This shouldn't take more than a week, during which time you two are to play the distraught parents of a kidnapped teen."

Dad elbowed Mom. "The role of a lifetime, hon." She ignored him.

John sat down in the chair across from Steven's desk and folded his arms as if he were done and quite satisfied with himself. "So, I guess that's it. As soon as we assign someone to Farrah, they'll be off."

Steven, quiet until now, got up and walked around his desk. "John, I think I am going to give you the job this time."

John was really surprised. Hadn't they ever let him out of the building? "But, sir, I'm not . . . I'm only . . ."

"You're the perfect guy for the job. Now all of you say your goodbyes and get out of here."

I'D RATHER BE HOME IN BED

AS IT TURNS OUT, THE FEDERAL Building on Wilshire Boulevard is a hub for hideouts all over the West Coast. When John and I were ready to leave, we were escorted to a fourth elevator bank that took us to the twelfth floor, no stops. We were silent as we rode up with a uniformed security person who was acting like he was protecting an armored car full of cash. His eyes darted right, then left, then right again, as he scanned the moving elevator car for intruders. When the doors opened, he motioned for us to stay inside until he had visually checked the area. Having satisfied himself, he stepped aside so that we could walk out into yet another lobby.

A middle-aged woman in a navy suit stood to greet us. "I am Hannah Devine, and you must be Farrah and John." John and I smiled and nodded and shook her hand like a couple of trained monkeys. It occurred to me just then that John knew nearly as little about what to expect as I did. He'd probably heard about where we were headed, but this was his first field assignment. "I was charged with assembling your survival kits, but frankly I've rarely been given so little time. I hope you find everything to your satisfaction, and if you need any—Oh, it's time for you to leave now." She turned to see the frame on the door behind her light up into a bright red.

The mute security guy pushed the door open and quickly pressed his thumb into the print reader on the inside wall to hold it open. He motioned for us to hurry up, so we each grabbed a small black duffle bag from Hannah's outstretched arms and followed him. He keyed some numbers into the pad above the print reader and the door slammed shut. A few more numbers and a pair of metal elevator doors slid out of the walls and met to completely enclose us in a silver box. The security guy spoke for the first time. "You might want to hold on to something."

I lightly grasped the handrail behind me, and John did the same. He rolled his eyes at me, the first sign of levity since we'd identified Creepy. The elevator started to descend, a little more quickly than normal. Then it started to accelerate so fast that I was sure we were no longer connected to any elevator cables at all. And how could we be falling so far? We'd only gone up to the twelfth floor.

We stopped abruptly, and I stumbled a little. John grabbed my upper arm to steady me and then immediately let go. We started moving again, this time sideways and fast, like we were on a train.

John wasn't surprised about this at all. "We have entered the Subterranean Transport Network. We are about a half mile below-ground. This elevator car will now take us to our secure location."

"Which is . . . ?"

"I forgot to ask." John cleared his throat to get the attention of the security guy. "Um, sorry, I forgot to ask. Where exactly will we be hiding?"

"I have been instructed to leave you in an interior compartment of building six in sector 312."

John shrugged and translated, "Downtown L.A., abandoned warehouse. It won't be terribly comfortable, but they'll never look there."

"It's also my responsibility to collect any traceable electronic devices at this point. FBI-issued cell phones are fine, but any others must be relinquished at this time."

John turned to me. "You have a cell phone?"

Hmmm. Yes. "No, I left it at home." I was on my way to

some mystery hideout for God knew how long. I wasn't about to relinquish my oak tree photo and end up in a straitjacket. I made a mental note to put it on airplane mode as soon as we got there. I leaned back against the elevator wall and reached into my back pocket to switch it to vibrate.

After about thirty minutes, the elevator stopped and started to move up toward sea level. When the doors opened, we were in a windowless, rectangular room, maybe twelve by eight feet. The security guy held the doors open for us to cross the threshold and started to show us around. There were two mismatched upholstered chairs in front of an old TV, a small table between the chairs, and literally nothing else. With a flourish, he opened a small cupboard with two deflated twin-size blow-up mattresses and two sleeping bags. "Would you like turndown service now, or would you like to do it yourself later?"

Ah, everyone's a comedian, even the security guy. He and John shared a little chuckle at his joke, like this was our honeymoon suite at some fine hotel. It was actually pretty funny, but in spite of myself I turned bright red. I hadn't quite thought this whole thing through logistically. Was I going to be shacked up with John in a windowless room, sleeping next to him and sharing a bathroom? Was this even legal? I'm sure my parents must have thought of this and had decided to trust him. But based on what, a thirty-minute meeting?

They were both looking at me, no longer laughing and potentially reading my mind. "Farrah, we are only going to be here for a week or so. I know it's grim, but the only thing that matters is that you are safe." John sounded like he was reading from a script.

"Sure. And do we get rations of dried food and Tang?" I was mostly trying to change the subject, but it was a legitimate concern.

Security guy smiled. "No, that part's pretty good. The elevator car that brought us here will come by three times a day, unmanned, and deliver food and documents as necessary. John, you can just text special requests to 4352, and depending on who's running the kitchen, you might get lucky. Other stuff like toothpaste and clean underwear should be in your survival bags."

I was red again. *Did that guy say "underwear"? Am I going to have to discuss my personal hygiene with these people?* My mind raced through all the possibilities for mortification.

Security guy shook John's hand as he got back into the elevator, a bellhop just looking for a tip from the newlyweds. "Nighty-night." Ugh.

John could tell I was about to freak out, so he tried to make everything seem really normal. "Wanna watch TV? Or should we just go to sleep? I'll put it on and then see if I can get in touch with the kitchen. Do you want a snack or anything?" I could tell by the tone in his voice, sort of the way you talk to a puppy, that he was terrified that I was going to start to cry again.

I got my mattress, pressed the green button for automatic blow-up, lay down, and pretended to sleep until I eventually did.

IF REALITY WANTS TO GET IN TOUCH,
IT KNOWS WHERE I AM

So that's how I ended up in this warehouse, sitting on this understuffed chair, watching the news break about my kidnapping on an antique TV. John was sitting on the other chair, taking in the rest of the five o'clock news. He switched the channel to another network to catch the tail end of my mom's dramatic exit back into the house.

"She seems more like a Farrah than you do."

"Everyone seems more like a Farrah than I do. It's called irony, and the best part is that she's named Rebecca. Wouldn't I have made a better Rebecca?"

"Natalie."

"What?"

"You seem more like a Natalie to me. Like Natalie Wood or Natalie Cole, a little more mysterious."

That's the last word I'd ever use to describe myself because for the past eight hours every thought I have jumps right on the brain slide and flies out of my mouth. Like right now, for instance: "It seems to me that ever since I failed to stop eight people from being blown up, every thought I have flies right out of my mouth. I suspect it's shock, but I wouldn't call it mysterious."

"I don't know. There's something mysterious about you; maybe you don't even know it. I don't meet a lot of kids who spend their spare time hunting terrorists."

Kids. Did he have to keep saying that? There I was in my best-fitting jeans with my best-fitting white T-shirt about to lie down and go to sleep next to a twenty-one-year-old man for God's sake! I felt less like a kid than I ever had.

After we'd finished a Coke, a turkey sandwich, and three episodes of *Everybody Loves Raymond,* the reality of our situation started to sink in. This had been the first day of who knew how many that we were going to be stuck in that room. I looked around at the four gray walls, the corner bathroom complete with both a toilet and a sink, and our two makeshift beds. It was a little hopeless.

"Wanna play cards?" John reached for his survival pack — really just a duffle bag, but I imagined there were tons of Bondesque gadgets in there. A deck of cards seemed a little low-tech.

"I'll play gin." He dealt us each seven cards on the tiny table between our chairs. I tried to adapt, as I am a ten-card gin player, well, since I was three. We played silently, one word uttered every five minutes or so: "Gin."

After I'd beat him twelve times in a row, he put his cards down and looked at me suspiciously. "You count cards too?"

"It's not different from any other random pattern. I mean remembering a sequence of numbers, colors, and letters that has passed by leads you to a probability of what the next card is going to be. It's really pretty easy. For me." I was surprising myself. I would normally have let someone beat me at gin to avoid having this conversation. Especially someone who was becoming more relaxed and a tad bit hotter every second. But don't get any ideas — it's not as if I had suddenly experienced some metamorphosis and, like a caterpillar breaking free to reveal its true nature as a butterfly, I was finally being my true Self. It's more like I'd already let my SAT scores out of the bag, and I knew I was going to be stuck here for a while. I didn't want to beat the terrorists to the punch by dying of boredom.

"It's all so crazy, isn't it?" I was kind of thinking out loud.

"I agree it is all crazy. But which part are you talking about?"

"The terrorists wanting to kill me. So that I won't stop them from protecting life. I guess a forest or a stream is more defenseless than I am, but not by much. I mean, how many people do they have to kill to save the planet?"

John shrugged. "I don't know, but we're doing a lot of damage. I read that Americans are using like 21 million barrels of oil every day. We're going to blow through a lot of resources in the next ten years."

"We are about 309 million Americans with a population growing at 1 percent a year. So that'll be 341 million people using 23 million barrels of oil per day in ten years." It sort of slipped out.

John stared at me in amazement. "Do you hire yourself out for parties?"

"Yep, that's why they call me Party Girl." I laughed for the first time, even though it was at my own inside joke. This was sort of fun, showing off for a person who wasn't my dad.

I got up and paced back and forth across our cell, which took exactly six steps in either direction. "Can we go outside? Is there a roof deck or anywhere we can breathe for a second?"

John raised an eyebrow. "Yes, welcome to the St. Regis Hotel. Please take the far elevator bank to the Rooftop Lounge, where our host will meet you to freshen up your drink and slit your throat . . ."

I stopped pacing and my hand darted up to my neck. John softened a bit. "Hey, Farrah, I'm sorry, but this is serious. We're not on a sleepover here. The guys who are looking for us have hunted and killed a lot of people."

I sat back down in my chair, silent. Neither of us was sure if I was going to cry, but we both knew that he hadn't needed to bring that up again.

Who knew the threat of tears could terrify a guy? John got up and grabbed our sleeping bags in one hand and fresh

Cokes in the other. "There must be a fire escape off the exterior room there. Let's sneak out for a second, then we'll come in and get some sleep." We walked through the only door in our cell into a huge exterior space with floor-to-ceiling windows that offered a view of another warehouse. I wondered how many people the FBI had holed up in these buildings; if we'd see another fugitive sneaking out for a little sanity.

John pulled up the rusty window and climbed through first. He held his hand out to me to help me through. The sun was setting, and it was getting cooler as we leaned back against the metal bars, pulling our knees up to our chins. John wrapped my sleeping bag around my shoulders, and I half thought he might keep his arm around me. It was a weird moment of noisy internal panic: *Is he making a pass at me? Gross, he's like an adult. Am I even safe here? Who does this guy think he is? Oh no!! He's taking his arm away! Please put your arm around me, pleeeeeease.*

"Are you excited about MIT?" John was making casual conversation, but it took me off-guard to hear it said out loud.

"I guess. It's a long way from Santa Monica, in every possible way. So, I guess so."

"You'll love it." John was looking out into the alley below us, scanning for I don't know what.

"How'd you finish college so fast?"

He took a long sip of his Coke and smiled at me. "I don't know. Maybe I'm not just a pretty face either."

I smiled, a little embarrassed, and started scanning the alley for nothing too, while I thought about my new favorite word: *either*. He could have just said, "I'm not just a pretty face." But he added *either*. *Either* can be an adjective (*I could lean over and kiss either his neck or his lips*), a pronoun (*His neck or his lips? Either will do*), or, like here, an adverb following a negative subordinate clause (*I'm not just a pretty face either*). I wondered if it could be a name. We could have a daughter and call her Either.

I could feel him watching me and hoped I'd kept my mouth shut during that last bit of craziness. I turned to him quickly to check. "What!?"

"Nothing." A cold wind blew between the buildings, and he pulled the sleeping bag tighter and shivered a little.

"Are you picking up Steven's shoulder shudder there?" I said, laughing.

He was trying not to smile. "Ouch, that's harsh. The guy's been through a lot."

"Like what? Schoolyard bullying?" Is it possible to have a really attractive neck? I'd never noticed anyone's neck in my life, and now I could not stop staring at this one.

The head on top of the neck was talking. "No, seriously, that thing he does is some sort of a post-traumatic tic. It's a really bad story. You sure you want to hear it?"

I knew I was going to feel either really bad or really terrified. So, no. "Okay."

"His first job at the FBI was on a task force to build weapons testing centers in the Southwest. He found a desert location where he figured they could do a little weapons testing without bothering anyone, not realizing that the desert is its own ecosystem and that Jonas Furnis was watching. The story goes that after the first day of testing, he was kidnapped from his bed and was kept prisoner for eighteen months. He was tortured brutally. They voluntarily freed him in the end, but not before they'd put him through months of electroshock therapy and cut off all of his fingers on his left hand. When he came back, he was doing that shudder thing all the time."

"All his fingers? Why?"

"I don't know really. Consensus around the FBI was always that it was to remind him not to identify them. Almost poetic, like we'll make sure you can't point the finger at us."

"Did you make that up?"

He laughed. "No, I couldn't make up something that dumb

and live with myself." He was quiet for a second and drained the last sip of his Coke. "But really, seriously, Steven is a nice guy and I guess a hero."

We sat in silence for a while. I played through my initial hilarity at Steven's weird tic, mentally kicking myself for the tenth time that week. Who did I think I was busting on a former terror hostage when chances were pretty good that I was next? I tried to imagine what Steven had been through, the kidnapping, the torture, and the likelihood of it happening to me. At least until I got completely distracted by John's right forearm. It was strong but not veiny in a Mr. Universe kind of way. And had just the right amount of hair to suggest he has fully completed puberty but not enough to suggest a square yard of carpet on his back.

John broke the silence. "I guess Steven was never able to finger his captors."

"Ha-ha."

"He could never point them out."

"Cute."

"He wasn't playing with a full hand."

"Stop, please."

"The whole thing's hard to grasp, right?"

"Well, now I know how he felt. Held captive by the corniest person in the world."

"Point taken."

Ugh.

SO, WHEN'S THE WIZARD GOING TO GET BACK TO YOU ABOUT THAT BRAIN?

A REPORTER WAS TALKING IN VOICE-OVER as the camera panned the front entrance to my high school. "Local Santa Monica High School senior Farrah Higgins, seventeen, has now been missing for more than twenty-four hours. Experts say that the first twenty-four hours of an abduction are critical and that the likelihood of recovering the victim alive declines significantly after that time."

Switch to smiling reporter. "Cliff Townsend here at school with several of Farrah's classmates." Olive, Veronica, Tish, and Kat are standing (or is *posing* a better word?) next to the school entrance. "Girls, what can you tell me about Farrah? Did you suspect that she was being followed? Did she have any new acquaintances?"

"Acquaintances?" Veronica was stumped.

"Friends," clarified the reporter.

"Oh, well, not that we knew. She hung out with us a lot. She was a little brainy but normal," said Kat.

"Did you notice any erratic behavior?" Veronica's face went blank again, so the reporter went on. "Anything different from normal?"

"Well yeah, there was that weird thing in Schulte's class, where Mr. Schulte was upset and she ran out of class." The proverbial light bulb, though dim in this group, lit up over Olive's head.

Veronica caught on. "That was really strange, or erotic as you say. Plus I heard he called her at home after that."

Kat finally got it. "And she missed school for the rest of the week. Has anyone like even questioned him?"

Cliff looked back into the camera, looking like he'd cracked the case. "You heard it here. Potential foul play in the disappearance of the Higgins girl. Leaves parents wondering how safe their children are at even the toniest of public schools. Back to you, Allison."

DON'T YA THINK HARD WORK MUST
HAVE KILLED SOMEONE?

↻

ON OUR SECOND FULL DAY OF captivity, the first set of documents arrived with cold toast and warm yogurt. We had two cups of gas station coffee with powdered milk and Sweet 'n Low. While the food was disgusting, the documents gave us a renewed sense of purpose — in short, something to do.

"We might as well dig in," John said, running his fingers through his nearly dirty hair. "If not into the food, then into these." He picked up an accordion file full of paper. Not stapled, not binder-clipped, not even rubber-banded to suggest order or segments. It was a mess. Dig in was all we could do.

I gulped down a bit of yucky coffee and boldly announced, "I'll start." But as I began with the first page and then flipped through the rest, I was shocked to see gibberish. They were all in some sort, or several sorts, of European, Middle Eastern, and Slavic languages. "What are we supposed to do with this stuff?"

"I think the plan is that I translate and you decode." John reached across our uneaten breakfast and took the pile from my hands.

"How are you going to do that? Did they send an FBI language decoder ring?"

"I speak most of these languages. I traveled a lot as a kid."

He didn't look up. I recognized in him that spark of diving into something you love. It was as if I were no longer there. Which of course made him all the more attractive.

"Why?"

"It's a long story. Let me get a few of these translated. These are mostly in Portuguese, Czech, and Farsi, and then you can do your thing." All business.

"But how could you . . . ?" I gave up. I didn't want to disturb him by turning on the TV, so I decided to try for a little personal hygiene. I crammed myself into the tiny bathroom and washed my face and brushed my teeth. I undressed and washed myself as well as I could with a sink full of lukewarm water and a small washcloth. We seemed to be sharing a bar of soap that had both an industrial fragrance and a prior owner. Could the FBI have coughed up a new bar of soap for our efforts?

When I was done, I got dressed and lay back on my sleeping bag, watching John work and playing math games in my head. I wondered how many cubic inches of air it took to fill a room that was twelve by six feet, adding in the two-by-three-foot bathroom and subtracting for the three pieces of furniture and the masses of our bodies.

Just as I was close to the answer, my back pocket started to vibrate. I nearly jumped, hoping that John hadn't heard that faint *zzzzz* sound. Who in the world would be calling a kidnapped girl? I got up and went back into the bathroom to check it out.

"Olive Grossman Text." I stared at my phone for a few seconds like it was going to bite me. Was this an old text coming in, or was she seriously texting me to crack the kidnapping case? I opened the text and read, *I think this is bullshit. Where are u?* I started to write back, *No. No. The kidnapping is legit. Promise.* But I couldn't be texting her if I was really bound and gagged somewhere. So I just turned off my phone and hoped she'd lose interest.

John looked up as I came out of the bathroom. "You're good to go."

"Can't the FBI get a computer program to do the translating?" I was looking through the sheets of handwritten translations he'd given me and noticed his odd but highly regular printing. Everything about it was so uniform that it almost looked as if it could be its own font. I could imagine it on the big list of fonts on my laptop: John Bennett Bold.

"They can and they do. But conversations like these are really hard to translate that way. They are so conversational and the people speak so heavily in idioms that you really need a translator who has spent time in the specific area."

"Like what?" I couldn't get my head around the fact that he knew all these languages. I felt like quizzing him, but he wasn't in the mood to be made a show of.

"I can't think of one. You get started, and I'll translate the next batch." I decided to stay on my "bed" to read. John had commandeered the food crate for his feet, and I had no other place to recline.

The documents were transcripts from intercepted cell phone conversations. I expected to read this:

Bad Guy 1: So we're all set. I've got the dynamite, and you bring the matches.
Bad Guy 2: Terminal Eight, JFK, see you there at ten a.m.
Bad Guy 1: Bye-bye.
Bad Guy 2: Later.

Not exactly. I started reading through the most mundane conversations ever. "Honey, will you pick up my dry cleaning?" (Evil dry cleaning?) "Basketball practice was changed to Wednesday night." (Explosive basketballs?) "They have heirloom tomatoes at the bodega on Seventy-seventh and Lexington." (Rocket launcher tomatoes?) . . . Seriously.

John was still furiously translating, like this all meant

something. After about twenty pages, I had to ask: "What are we doing?"

Not looking up. "It's a process. We have to get through these and look for some kind of code. These guys know they are being monitored, so they have to speak in code. Isn't that what you do?" Now he was looking at me, and I started feeling a little defensive.

"What I do? I go to school; I go to parties. Let's not start saying this is what I do. I didn't ask for this."

Half smile. Zing. "Back to work, Buffy. Time to leave the mall and figure out how to stop the vampires."

Ha-ha. I decided to try. If heirloom tomatoes were bombs and the bodega was a bomb-making place (probably not the technical term), then they were on sale?

Day two went on like this, with me searching for something that wasn't there. He translated pages and passed them to me. I read them, saw nothing of note, and placed them in an orderly pile. I waited for more pages and monitored the crease between his dark eyebrows, his utter concentration. The brow gave way to his wide dark eyes, which sat on the cheekbones, which led to the jaw, which acted as a frame for his perfect lips. Had I gone mad?

My brain had obviously been compromised. I didn't know if it was the crappy food, the lack of sleep, the threat to my life, or some narcotic being pumped into our cell. But at the end of the day, I knew I had to regroup. He'd barely looked at me all day, and I was fabricating some kind of mad crush. Enough.

"I'm going to sleep. More tomorrow." I went to the other side of our tiny room and arranged my air mattress against the wall. I got in my sleeping bag and took mental inventory of the situation. I was sleeping in my clothes; I needed a shower; I was hungry—but not hungry enough to eat another turkey sandwich. And I was having a strangely fun time.

I pulled my sleeping bag over my head and turned on my phone, just to make sure it was still charged.

Olive Grossman Text (4):

1. I went to your house yesterday to see your parents. Danny was by the pool totally relaxed. And I'm supposed to think you're kidnapped?!

2. Kat thinks you're in rehab.

3. Danny told me not to worry about you and we swam. I wore your blue bikini, love it!

4. Wore it home, btw. Give it to you when you get back. Ur coming back, right?

Three more days passed as the crack crime-fighting team of Farrah and John got nothing but the giggles. All the documents were translated, and we read them over and over, eventually acting out the conversations like we were in the fifth grade play. A few more days of this and I was sure we'd be in a full-blown musical production of *Terror in Terminal 8.*

> *Farrah: No, I didn't hear about the schedule change.*
> *John: Well, they e-mailed you . . .*
> *Farrah: You can't expect me to run home and check my e-mail in the middle of the day.*

Scintillating theater. We read the transcripts of two old guys talking about how the entrance to the park had been closed off at Seventy-sixth Street that morning. We were a mother and a son talking about the cousin who showed up for Sunday dinner looking a little high. John read his parts with different accents to keep them fresh. So what had started as Czech had turned into a middle-class Brit or an Oklahoma oil baron. In short, we were getting nowhere.

Our favorites were Scarlet and Luke, who were in the

throes of a secret romance and speaking Portuguese. There seemed to be someone named Britney (I am *not* making this up—John translated it into the spelling of the troubled diva herself), who was helping them sneak around. It read like a romance novel, and we were really getting into it.

Scarlet: Hey. I was hoping you'd call.
Luke: Can you talk?
Scarlet: When can I see you? I really think this is the right thing. I can't think about anything else.
Luke: So you've made up your mind?
Scarlet: Yes. I'll try to come see you tonight, but if I can't get there, don't think it's because I'm not committed.

On and on this goes. By the seventh transcript, we'd gotten through five weeks of these conversations. They'd met out several times, never saying where. Britney knew all about it, but they seemed a little paranoid about being followed. At the bottom of Scarlet and Luke's transcripts, there was the tag "UES, NYC," and the time of day. John clued me in that UES was Upper East Side, pleased that he'd cracked it and I hadn't. What did I know? I'd never been east of Arizona.

Scarlet: I really need to see you.
Luke: What's wrong?
Scarlet: There's something going on with Britney. She's a cheater. We can't trust her anymore.
Luke: Of course, she's a cheater—that's her whole game. Why are you acting like that's news?
Scarlet: Because now she's cheating on us. Britney's a first-class slut, and I can prove it.
Luke: You can?
Scarlet: Enough to get her messed up for good. I found it in an e-mail; she sent it to try to show me how much support there is for what we're doing. But it shows a lot more than

that. I'll give you what I have, but I have to explain it to you. I think there's a way we can use it to take care of those left behind.

Luke: Shhh, honey.

Scarlet: Right. Meet me at seven.

Later . . .

Luke: Where were you? I waited until nine!

Scarlet: They're watching and listening all the time. I don't know when I'm going to be able to meet you.

Luke: You have something to give me. Proof.

Scarlet: Of course, it's packed up. You'll have it.

Luke: Are you crying?

Scarlet: I'm fine. It's just . . . just that I have it all packed in his diaper bag. It contains everything you'll need to take care of him after I'm . . .

Luke: Careful, honey.

Scarlet: Sorry.

John and I had moved our armchairs together, sharing the food crate as a footrest and awkwardly leaning in so we could both read the transcript at the same time. I took the pages and straightened them on my lap. "This kind of flies off the rails as a newly blossoming love story. There's a baby? And a diaper bag? Full of what? Diapers?"

John got up to stretch his legs. We'd been reading for hours without a break. "Probably full of evidence against Britney. And I agree—the drama is too high even for new romance. And all of a sudden he's calling her 'honey'?"

We gave up for the day and decided to go to bed. We took turns in the bathroom and crawled into our sleeping bags on top of our air mattresses. The past few nights we'd both immediately turned to face away from each other, a weak grasp at privacy. But that night I didn't hear him turn. I flipped back over to find him lying on his back, head resting in hands, staring at the dark ceiling. "Aren't you going to sleep?" Great, I'm his mother now.

"I'm just thinking about Scarlet."

Creepy. "What about her?"

"Not her really, as much as her name. It's probably because I just really want it to be her, you know to solve this thing, but Scarlet is just such a good name for a suicide bomber."

I wondered what Farrah was a good name for. "Is that like a thing in the baby books? Suicide bomber names?"

He laughed and turned over to look at me. "It's just kind of a violent name. Like the color of blood. In the Bible it's used to symbolize sin, and in *The Scarlet Letter* too. Or in mythology it's the color of the Phoenix's wings. And a suicide bomber is a little like a Phoenix, right?"

Uh, hello, clueless here. "The Phoenix's wings? Because they fly and . . . the bombing was at the airport?"

He laughed again. I wasn't sure if it was because I was becoming increasingly goofy or what, but he'd been laughing a lot more easily. "No, the Phoenix is a mythological bird, a fire spirit, with scarlet wings and a gold tail. It lives for like five hundred years and then builds itself a nest that bursts into flames. The Phoenix and the nest burn violently until they are just ashes. And from the ashes comes a new Phoenix, gloriously reborn. I guess it's just the deliberate burning of oneself for a cause. And the scarlet wings."

"It sounds like a stretch, but I like the story." We lay there looking at each other in the dark, then looking away because we'd been looking at each other. I'll have to measure it, but there is an exact amount of time you can look at someone silently before it's weird.

John kept talking. "Or Dido . . ."

"Who?"

"That would be another one for your baby book of suicide bomber names. Dido? You know who burned herself on a pyre? After Aeneas left her? Nothing?" I shook my head. "Okay, good night, Fa . . . Does anyone ever call you anything besides Farrah?"

"Nope."

"Okay, good night . . ."

In the morning we got back to work. We assumed our regular positions in our armchairs, sipped our coffee, and started reading. There were tons of pages of these conversations, most of them romantic, making and then canceling plans to meet. Scarlet seemed a lot more into Luke than he was into her, if you ask me. The final transcripts got a little desperate. It seemed like they'd been unable to meet for a while and Scarlet was freaking out.

> *Scarlet: Where have you been?*
> *Luke: It's been impossible to call.*
> *Scarlet: I've talked to Britney. She knows we know. I'll explain it all when I see you. But she's terrified and has agreed to pay. This all falls on you now. You'll have to get the money where it needs to go. You have to promise me.*
> *Luke: You know I will. I know how to reach them. You just have to get me the bag.*
> *Scarlet: Oh, honey, I can't stop thinking about seeing you. I have to make that happen.*
> *Luke: I know.*
> *Scarlet: I keep remembering the night we walked down Grace Church Street, holding hands and looking up at the city lights. I loved being with you then.*
> *Luke: Uh-huh. I love you too, but what about the bag?*
> *Scarlet: And now I think about that night and wish I were back there, but without all the burdens I am carrying around. I feel so lost when I am not with you. I just really need to release the past and find a future with you.*
> *Luke: Yeah, honey. Me too.*

Scarlet: You're not listening to me! You have to listen. I am lost without you; we have to find more time together. Do you hear me?
Luke: I'm out of time here. I have to hang up.

John started laughing and was definitely messing up the moment. He delivered all of Luke's lines while placing an imaginary gun to his head. "I'm sorry, but I'm really starting to hope these people are terrorists. They're obviously blackmailing Britney with whatever's in that bag. But what is all this random where-are-we-going-let's-analyze-our-relationship talk? I've heard my fair share of this stuff, and this isn't how it sounds in real life."

Really? Because you've had a lot of relationships with desperate women? Like, are you in one now? And are we defining a desperate person as one who really needs you to sit back down in your chair so that your forearm might have the chance to come within a half inch of mine while we read?? Because I can feel that, just so you know.

"That's not fair. She's having a hard time. They can't be together, and they're in love. Maybe." I don't know why I was getting so protective about Scarlet. Or why I was clinging to this obviously fake romance. She didn't seem like love-struck/desperate, more like desperate/desperate. I decided to try to make poor Scarlet seem a little cooler by saying her lines in my coolest, most indifferent tone. But she wasn't helping at all.

By night six we'd gotten a new box of documents, roast beef sandwiches on rye (rejoice!), a Corona with a lime for John, and a Coke for me. We celebrated by doing all of our reading on the fire escape.

Scarlet: I can't go through with it. I just feel so selfish.
Luke: Listen to me, they're so close to finding us out, you have to act now. Remember you are doing it for the baby, for all babies.

"This is getting so heavy." I was really starting to feel like I knew these people. "What is this baby? This makes no sense.

Even if she is a suicide bomber, what kind of terrorist blows up a family to save the children?"

"I know, but there's more. Keep going. Get to the ones that are time stamped 0700 on the morning of the suicide bombing." Because John had done the translating, he was always one step ahead of me. Annoying.

Scarlet: I just can't believe this is how it's going to end. You can go get the bag.

Luke: That's my girl. Now listen carefully and I'll tell you where to drop it.

Scarlet: I already told you where I'd drop it. It's already there. And my ride's here. I have to go. I'm out of time. You idiot, you wouldn't be able to read it, anyway. I thought you were a professional.

"A professional? Then what?" I wanted to rip the pages from his hands. Was he really going to keep the end of this story from me?

"That's it. All contact ends there at seven a.m. on the morning of the bombings. This has to be them."

"We missed something about the bag."

"And so did Luke."

"Okay, I'll admit this doesn't make sense as a romantic drama. And there's some sort of evidence against Britney in that bag. Who's probably a terrorist too, right?"

"But she says Luke wouldn't be able to read it without her."

"So she's the brains of the operation."

John gave me a sideways smile and clinked his Corona bottle against my Coke. "Poor Luke. I know just how inadequate he feels."

"Ha-ha." I knew he was kidding. We'd been complete partners over the past few days. I bet he'd never felt inadequate once in his whole life.

We were both staring down into the alley for answers, a habit of ours since there was really no place else to look on the fire escape, except at each other. We'd learned the hard way that, given the width of the fire escape, if we both turned our heads toward each other at the same time, we were practically nose to nose. As appealing as the idea was, I slipped into a panic each time it happened, quickly turning back to watch the alley like it was my job.

After a while I said, "So, is it time to call Steven and tell him that we've caught the bad guys? How does that work?"

"Feels like it, right? But there's so much evidence that points to them, and really no evidence at all. I mean, it fits that it could be them, but it could also be that they are having an office romance and they found an e-mail linking Britney to the male receptionist, so now they are going to blackmail her into giving the whole office an extra week of vacation after they've quit."

"Yeah, John. That's probably it." I rolled my eyes and went back to work staring at the alley.

"I know it's them, but the information ends here. We have no more transcripts. We need the bag. Even if we call Steven, there's no place to go from here. Unless there's forensic evidence that we don't know about at the crime scene?" He shrugged hopefully and pulled out his phone to call Helen, Steven's assistant.

"Could you look and see if there is any information not released to the press about the suicide bomber? Yeah, use my password. Sure, take your time. That's it? Okay. Thanks."

Sounded like a dead end again, but John was smiling. I mean full smile: both corners of his mouth up, eyes sparkling, smiling.

"What? There's no information, right?"

"That's not exactly what she said. She said the bomber had been posing as a flight attendant. And the only thing left of her was her right foot. It had a Phoenix tattooed on the ankle. Nothing else.'"

"*Her* right foot? With a Phoenix. What are the chances?"

"Scarlet was definitely our suicide bomber. We've got to find that diaper bag."

IT DOESN'T TAKE A GENIUS TO SPOT
A GOAT IN A FLOCK OF SHEEP

WE STAYED UP LATE THAT NIGHT. We pushed our air mattresses together and lay down, passing pages back and forth, looking for the conversation where she told him where she was going to put the diaper bag. At least where she thought she told him. And if we were right, Luke never figured it out—not having the benefit of the complete transcripts of their conversations and nothing else in the world to do but review them—and the bag was still where she left it.

John put the transcripts down and propped himself toward me on his elbow. "Okay, let's review what we know. Scarlet and Luke are pretending to be lovers for the sake of whoever is listening. Someone named Britney has been helping them with whatever they're doing, but Scarlet has turned against her because of something she's found out about her in an e-mail that Britney sent her. And she has proof of whatever Britney did wrong that she's using as blackmail and plans to hand over to Luke. In a diaper bag."

"Right. And she'd need Britney to pay Luke, because Scarlet was going to be dead. And Luke was going to use the money to take care of someone. But Luke needs the bag to keep blackmailing Britney. And then on the morning of the bombing, Luke is going to tell her where to leave it for him. But Scarlet is pissed because she already told him where she was leaving it."

John gave me the transcripts, lay back down so we were head to head, and told me to keep reading. We murmured under our breath as we read. "Miss you, meet me, love you, the baby, blah-blah . . ."

"Poor Luke. I bet he's feeling like a real jackass right about now for not listening to his woman." John sounded like he was half kidding.

Of course. "That's it. Give me the last thirty pages. Remember at the beginning when they were seeing each other all the time, their conversations were more relaxed in a I'll-tell-you-later sort of way? And then at the end when they couldn't see each other, there was all that relationship babble? It was all so random, and she was mad because she felt like he wasn't listening. There's got to be something in there."

I went through that conversation again and again. "Try to see if you can get a Google map of Grace Church Street in any borough of New York City."

He pulled out his phone. "None."

"Expand it further."

"Okay, there's a Grace Church Street in Westchester County. It's the suburbs outside of New York City."

"So is the bag there? Sitting on a suburban street? That doesn't make any sense, plus she said they were looking at the city lights."

"I've been to Westchester — it's all trees, no lights."

I threw my papers on my bed. "I don't know. I'm going to take a 'shower.'" It's true that I made air quotes every time I mentioned the showerless closet in the corner of the room with just a sink and a faucet that dribbled out tepid water. Toothpaste had been key, but better soap would have been welcome.

I had the water running and was hoping for a spontaneous hot water connection, when I got it. Not the hot water, but I got "it." I ran back to the transcript and plopped on my mattress.

"Quick 'shower.'" John fished for an explanation for this sudden change of heart.

"Grace Church Street. GCS. Grand Central Station. Do you guys ever pay attention to anything we say?" I was smiling now, because I knew I was close. I was a little kid with a 3-D puzzle of the Empire State Building, and I'd just found the last corner.

"Let's do this again." We both lay down on my mattress, and I held the transcript over our faces. "I'll read her lines again. 'I keep remembering the night we walked down Grace Church Street, holding hands and looking up at the city lights. I loved being with you then.'"

"Okay, could be the location drop, Grand Central Station, and then she moans about the relationship."

"Fine," I said. "Let me go on. 'And now I think about that night and wish I were back there, but without all the burdens I am carrying around. I feel so lost when I am not with you.' She wants to get rid of the burdens, maybe something she's sick of carrying around."

"Like the diaper bag."

"But where in Grand Central could she leave a bag unattended? The only other things she says are, 'I just really need to release the past and find a future with you.' And . . ." I thumbed through to find it. "Here. 'You have to listen. I am lost without you; we have to find more time together. Do you hear me?'"

The answer came to me so fast and in such a satisfying way that I threw my arms around John and shouted, "Got it!" a little too loudly in his ear.

He pried my hands from around his neck but kept them in his. He asked, "What now?"

"She's lost without him and wants to find a future with him. Get it? Lost and Found. She left the bag either on a train so it would be put in the Lost and Found, or she put it there herself. Call Helen. See how long stuff is kept in the Lost and Found in Grand Central."

John seemed surprised to realize he was still holding my hands. He muttered, "Sorry," and got up and called Helen and then Steven. I lay back on my mattress, supremely pleased with myself. When he hung up he said, "I've been sprung. Looks like I'm going to New York in the morning."

CRYBABY ON BOARD

"YOU? WHAT DO YOU MEAN *YOU*?" It took me a few seconds to really hear what he'd said.

"I've got clearance to leave. I'm getting out of here. Hot shower and a flight to New York to see if I can grab that bag." He was up now, walking around, throwing things in his duffle bag.

My throat closed. I wrapped my arms around myself, still in the spot where John and I had been working for days and even holding hands for ten seconds.

He stopped his packing and sat back down next to me. "Hey. I'm not going to leave you alone here. They'll send someone else to stay with you." A little nudge with his shoulder. "No one as cool as me. But they'll send someone."

It had taken a lot for me to feel comfortable here with John. Now I was going to start over again with who—the wise-cracking security guard? Super-stiff Hannah Devine? The truth was it didn't matter who they replaced him with—I really didn't want John to leave. I tried a withholding strategy: "If you go without me, I won't help you anymore. You'll get whatever's in that diaper bag, and you're on your own."

John smiled. "Farrah, I've got the whole FBI behind me. I'll be okay."

He had a point there. New strategy, a threat: "You'd better hope nothing happens to me. Protecting me was your first field assignment. What if I start screaming from the balcony and get found?"

"You wouldn't do that." Again, a good point.

I lowered myself to guilt: "And you'd really leave me here with just anyone? My parents trusted me with you, not Bruno from Sector Six." A little pause, I was getting somewhere.

He was quiet, his hands clasped in front of him as if praying for an answer. The answer came and he shook his head. "Anyone can keep you safe in here, Farrah. I have to go to New York. I'll come back with whatever that evidence is and get you out of here. Two days, tops."

I'm a little ashamed to admit what happened next, but I was out of ideas. I'd played to his sympathies, I'd played to his overly developed sense of duty, and I had one card left. It was a cheap shot, a sucker punch if you will. I knew very little about John (besides the exact outline of his jaw and the way it framed his mouth like rigid parentheses around a soft word that is too delicious to be spoken aloud—I'd noticed that). But I knew that he was not exactly comfortable swimming in even the shallow end of human emotions. So I started to cry.

My success in this area was unprecedented. I wondered, as he put his arm around me and reached for another clean hankie, if this mastery of the tear duct could take me to the White House. Or the altar. Must remember to use my powers for good, not evil. "Shhh," he was saying to me. "It's okay. Please stop. Shhh." He got up and, sadly, took his arm with him. He was pacing with his hands folded and under his chin, nodding to himself as he walked. I whimpered a little so as not to release him from my control.

"Seriously, Farrah. Please. Stop. I'm going to call Steven. Just let me think." Job done, I stopped. John had him on the phone immediately. "Listen, I think I need to take Farrah with me. I know. It is. But there is evidence in that bag, and the operative who left it there thought that her partner would not be able to decode it. I can go alone and bring it back to our guys or to Farrah, but it would be faster if she came with me. We could have it decoded tomorrow. I really think we . . . really? Yes, I agree. Okay. In the morning. Okay, bye."

He smiled at me. "Happy? Steven thinks you need to go with me too. He'll let your parents know, and we fly out in the morning." He sat down on his air mattress.

"Thanks. I swear I'm going to help." I wiped the last of my tears away and hoped it hadn't made me look all blotchy.

"No more crying?"

"No more making me cry?"

"Promise."

I ♥ NY

⌒

I SLEPT FOR ABOUT TWO HOURS before John woke me up. "Coffee's here, and security is coming for us in twenty minutes."

"Then let me sleep for eighteen minutes. It's not like I'm not already fully dressed." I turned over and pulled the sleeping bag over my head. John left me alone.

When the security guy got there, I was dead asleep again. His voice woke me up to the realization that we were actually getting out of there. I sprung up, brushed my teeth, grabbed my bag, and got in the elevator in a matter of two minutes. After retracing our steps through three elevators, we were back in Steven's office, where nothing seemed to have changed. Including our clothes.

"You two are going to have to see what you can find in New York and report directly to me. Don't deal with any local authority, call me." Uh, control freak?

Helen walked in and escorted us into the hallway. "If you are going to get to New York under everyone's radar, you're going to have to change your clothes. And, well, maybe, shower?"

"Thank God." I followed her to what amounted to the FBI's version of a high school locker room. Helen left me a brand-new bar of soap, a tiny bottle of shampoo, and a bag of clothes to change into.

The shower was a little bit of a disappointment, as the water never creeped above warm and automatically shut off every two minutes. But the soap and shampoo were nice. I dried off and looked in the mystery costume bag. Not bad. My disguise was as a businesswoman, with John as my colleague. I wore a black wool-blend suit, more blend than wool but nice. It was tailored to snip in at all the right places to ensure a promotion. The heels were higher than I would have picked, but I was going with it. How far could I possibly have to walk in New York City?

Fully dressed, I snuck into a bathroom stall and turned on my phone.

Olive Grossman Text (2):

1. At beach for sunset with Danny, he's still says you're totally kidnapped but laughs like it's funny. I'm not buying it. Just reply with one word to tell me I'm right.

2. P.S. I never knew Danny was so funny! ☺

It took all of my mental strength not to write back and demand to know why she's watching the sunset with my little brother. I turned off my phone and tucked it in my suit jacket pocket. It only had 20 percent battery power left.

John was waiting for me in his office, shaved and decked out in a second expensive suit (definitely not FBI issue), flipping through mail and stuff that had accumulated over the past few days. He looked up when I came in. "Wow. You're supposed to be my business partner? How's anyone at the office supposed to concentrate?"

Sweet. "Yeah it was easier for me to focus when you stunk too." Bold, right? I think my GCS success was going to my head. And I have to admit his light little flirtations were doing me a world of good, even if he meant them in a grandfatherly isn't-she-purdy sort of way.

My carry-on luggage was waiting for me, a discreet black gym bag with my jeans, favorite T-shirt, socks, and boots shoved in a stinky mess. Who says the government's inefficient? A black sedan with tinted windows dropped us at the JetBlue terminal, and we were in the air by eleven a.m.

We were seated in the last row of the coach cabin. Our seats didn't recline, but they were very convenient to the bathrooms. Gee, thanks. I fell into a fitful sleep almost as soon as the plane took off. When I woke up, John was on hour three of the National Geographic Channel. Shamelessly nerdy.

"Hungry?" John was watching me wake up and orient myself.

"Sure." He pulled out a couple of roast beef sandwiches from his carry-on and pulled my tray table down.

We ate in a comfortable silence for a while before he busted out with, "Do you have a boyfriend at home?"

I nearly spit out my last bite of roast beef. "What? No! I mean . . . no. Why are you asking that?"

"I was just thinking about it while I was watching you sleep. Your parents know where you are, and your friends seem a little too dumb to care. But I was wondering if there was some guy who is in love with you and wondering if you're okay. It just seems kind of cruel if there is."

This all seemed highly personal. "No boyfriend. I've never had a boyfriend. Or anything." I wondered if he fully understood how anything really meant *anything,* with the exception of the ill-fated pesto kiss. "I've never really been able to relate to a guy in that way, and you can imagine they'd probably think I was a little off if they got to know me."

He laughed. "A little off? Try way off the deep end." I gave him a punch in the arm, and he pretended it hurt. It was the best way I could think of to change the subject. Besides this:

"So do you have a girlfriend who's wondering where you are?"

"That's probably exactly why I don't have a girlfriend. I can never really tell anyone what I'm doing. I've gotten so good at keeping secrets that apparently I'm emotionally closed off. At least that's what I've heard. Repeatedly."

"Wow. I can totally see that. You've got some serious robot tendencies. I've just spent 168 hours with you straight, I've spilled all my deepest, darkest secrets, and I don't even know where you grew up. Weird."

"Those were your deepest, darkest secrets?" He was laughing at me again.

"Yeah, like my SAT scores? Those are in a sealed file at my school."

"Oh, okay." Then he said something that sounded like *"Kzhet jed swarky; shebedokrt shee,"* and laughed. "It's Ukrainian: 'My hut is on the edge of the village; I know nothing.' Like 'I'm not in the inner circle; your secret is safe with me.' Don't worry, I've got nothing that compares to perfect scores, but I've got my own stuff. I'm just used to keeping myself to myself. Why are we talking about this?"

"You brought it up. You were wondering about my heartbroken boyfriend and ended up 'fessing up to some serious intimacy issues."

He gave me a raised eyebrow. I had to defend myself. "I watch *Oprah*, I know."

We circled for thirty minutes before we could land at JFK. Apparently with all the added security and Terminal 8 being out of commission, the airport was a mess.

The elderly couple across the aisle from us was quickly losing patience. "Ridiculous. We'll never make our connection. This is the last time I make this trip." They tossed complaints back and forth between each other until they cycled on to repeats. "Ridiculous." They lobbed a few at John. "Can you believe this? We were supposed to land at seven. By the time they find us a gate, it'll be eight thirty."

"Yes, sir. I imagine the whole airport has slowed down." John seemed very young to me, politely addressing this old guy.

The wife leaned over her husband to address me. "I tell you, this is a total disaster. It will be months before this airport is functioning right."

"I know. I'm sorry." I meant it.

The wife laughed. "I can't imagine how it's your fault, dear, but thank you." They both fell silent, content that at least they'd gotten an apology.

At JFK we raced through Terminal 5, past armed military men, and hopped into a cab to Grand Central. "Aren't we going to check in to our hotel first?"

John smiled at me like I was cute. And seven. "They haven't let me know where we'll be spending the night yet. We'll get our work done first."

"You mean staying."

"What?"

"You meant to say, 'They haven't let us know where we are staying,' like to imply a hotel, with a minibar and a big bathtub and unlimited hot water. Right? The phrase 'spending the night' suggests, well, what we've been doing the past six nights. I smell an air mattress when I hear that."

"I meant spending the night. But we'll see what they say after we get the bag."

The city was just like I'd imagined it from TV and the movies. But bigger, taller, and louder. The traffic was slow, so we got out of our cab at Park Avenue and Fiftieth Street and walked seven blocks to Grand Central Station. I got half a block before I decided that women who could walk in heels must be professionally trained athletes. I teetered along beside John, stopping to fix my heel more than a few times. But no one saw me, no one noticed. You could really do anything in New York City.

We entered Grand Central Station through Vanderbilt Avenue and took the escalator to the Main Concourse. Riding down that escalator, next to John, I drank in the magic of what was around me. The ceiling was gold-leafed with a depiction of the constellations on it. The layout of the night sky was backwards, but perfectly backwards. If everything in New York was going to be that beautiful, I didn't care if it was all upside down.

John was looking at me. "You okay?"

"I love it."

"Me too. Let's go." Dream sequence over, back to work. Everything went so easily, that I started to wonder why it was so hard to get a job at the FBI. We asked at the Information booth where we could find the Lost and Found. We went there and looked through thirty-two bags until we found the one and only diaper bag. John threw it over his shoulder, and we walked out. Like shooting fish in a barrel, right? Wrong.

WHAT WOULD SCOOBY-DOO?

I WAS GIDDY WITH SUCCESS AND the realization that I had a future as a terror-fighting, high heel–wearing, code-breaking badass. John was noticeably less relaxed. He took my arm as we left Grand Central Station, scanning the Main Concourse like he was watching a tennis match. He led me up the main escalators and out onto Forty-third Street and Vanderbilt.

"John, they're not after us." I was teetering as he rushed me along. "They are probably still watching my house or the FBI parking lot. If they knew where their precious bag was, they would have grabbed it before we did or killed us already. Relax."

A cab jumped out of the taxi line and pulled right up alongside of us. I guessed it paid to be well-dressed in the big city. We got into the cab and the driver muttered, "Where to?"

"Please take us uptown to the Excelsior Hotel, Eighty-first and Central Park West."

We drove in silence across town, toward the West Side Highway. All the windows were down, and the cool spring air blew the sound of the horns and screeching brakes to make a symphony for my ears. We passed through Times Square, and I stuck my head out of the window to catch every light, every shimmer. It was like being in a big box made of Lite-Brites, but moving and magical. We passed four Broadway theaters with lines of well-dressed and not-so-well-dressed people clamoring to get in. I looked over to John, sure I would catch him watching my wonder with amusement. I was ready to defend my naiveté, but instead saw his profile with jaw clenched and brows furrowed in concentration. Did this guy have a problem giving his regards to Broadway?

I snuck a peek into the diaper bag. Inside I expected bombing tools, and what those were going to look like I had no idea. Instead I found a stack of maybe forty-five pages of computer paper, with columns of numbers.

"Anything?" John asked, still staring straight ahead.

I shook my head. "No, but it's a little more my speed than the romance babble."

We got onto the West Side Highway and headed uptown, the Hudson River and the lights of New Jersey in the distance. I couldn't take it anymore. I was having the time of my life, and he was such a dud. "Okay, are you going to relax now? We did it. It sounds like you're springing for a hotel and we're heading back to L.A. tomorrow. Right?"

"Shhh." Jeez. I couldn't figure out why he was so tense. Maybe he had big plans for our night at the hotel together? I mean, we had just spent seven solid days together, no breaks. We'd developed such an easy banter and an equally easy silence. We'd slept ten inches from each other every night and had worked two inches from each other every day. Why would he be nervous? Had I been playing too hard to get?

"I'm going to need you to change your shoes."

"Why? I like these. I mean, for sitting. I feel kind of . . ."

"Right now." He grabbed my gym bag, pulled out my cowboy boots, and pulled my heels off. This was a little sudden. The guy's had seven days to kiss me, and now he goes for my feet? In a cab? I pulled on my socks and boots obediently.

"Okay, you're kind of freaking me out."

He leaned in so close that I could feel his breath on my neck. In a flash I realized that my instincts had been right about these boots. I had worn them every day for four years, enduring my mother's pleas that I try a pair of wedges. I'd had them resoled six times, because on some level I'd known that these boots had special powers. I vowed right then and there to never take them off, to never let my foot grow another half size. He was about to kiss me, and I owed it all to my boots.

He spoke in a whisper in my ear: "I'm holding up three fingers, and when I count back to one, we are going to jump out of the cab onto the grass to our right. Do you understand?"

I heard: *I adore you, you're beautiful, and now I am going to kiss you like you've never been kissed before.* So when he threw open the taxi door and pulled me out onto the shoulder of the West Side Highway, and I felt myself crash into what passes for grass in New York City, let's just say I was a bit surprised.

John grabbed my hand and started running. Our taxi driver swerved to a stop, abandoned his car in the middle of the highway, and ran in our direction, screaming into his cell phone. This was all starting to make sense to me. Kiss? No. Death? Maybe.

We were ahead of him by about a block as we ran east across Riverside Drive. We were both fairly fast, except that we were carrying our gym bags and the now-all-important diaper bag. We ran down a long block of apartment buildings on Eighty-fourth Street, barely catching the attention of the doormen standing guard. I longed to run into one of those buildings to safety but knew that John wouldn't want to endanger the residents. We were running to get killed in solitude.

We crossed Columbus Avenue against the light and were nearly flattened by a downtown bus. The taxi driver was gaining on us, mainly because he was not schlepping luggage and was sporting slightly more sensible shoes. As we got closer to Central Park West, the streets were getting quieter and the taxi driver was getting closer. We would have been better off staying on the busier two-way streets where we could have ducked into restaurants or subway stations, but John was leading me, and I knew that wasn't how he wanted this to end. As it was, we were running down a fancier part of Eighty-fourth Street, quiet and tree-lined, toward Central Park. Which would be deserted.

The street was so quiet that I could hear the taxi driver's phone ring behind us. He must have looked down to answer it, because he missed John pushing me between two parked vans and flattening me face-down in the street.

I looked up in time to see the driver's feet run by in hot pursuit. Very Scooby-Doo, right? All I needed now was a sarcophagus to hide in and a really big sandwich. Silently, John pulled me up again and dragged me through an alley to Eighty-third Street. "We have about thirty seconds to get in another cab and get the hell out of here before he backtracks. Move!" We ran like mad into a crowd on Amsterdam Avenue. A taxi was waiting for a lady with two little kids who was struggling to fold up her stroller, keep the kids off the street, and send a text. We slipped into the other side of the taxi, John threw a fifty into the front seat, and we sped off before she could hit Send.

"Where to?"

"Please drive all the way downtown. In fact, take us to Brooklyn." He turned to me. "Are you okay?"

Since I didn't know the answer to that question specifically, I just started to ramble. "My arm hurts, and I might have a blister on my left toe because I put my socks on wrong, but that was good that you had me change my shoes or I'd be dead. Did that guy want to kill me or get the bag or both? What's in this bag, and how did you know that guy was going to try to kill us?" *And, believe it or not, I'm a little disappointed because I really thought you were going to kiss me in that cab while we zoomed along the Hudson River with no one but the city lights watching us.*

"Let me look at your arm." I took off my suit jacket, and he gently poked the newly forming bruise on my left arm. "It's going to be an ugly bruise, but it's nothing to worry about. And I don't know why you thought I was going to kiss you."

Hello?! Internal dialogue? Can you hear me now?! "I think you can see now how important the job is that I've been given. I am responsible for keeping you alive. And I nearly failed a few minutes ago. You are my charge, and I am an agent. I am an adult, and you are a minor. I could get fired or arrested, or worse. I am not going to kiss you. Clear?" He was all business; I was mortified.

"What's in Brooklyn?" My survival instincts told me I'd have to change the subject before I spontaneously combusted.

"Nothing. I just want to get away. This guy's okay," he said, motioning at the driver. "But that last guy was talking into his cell phone in a rare dialect of Russian, and he was speaking very cryptically. These past few days, you must have turned me into some sort of code cracker. He was checking in with someone and told them that he had us and that, yes, we had bags with us. He confirmed that he'd dispose of us and our belongings."

"He didn't want the diaper bag?"

"No, I think that guy was just out to kill you."

I looked out the window at the city lights as we zoomed back down the West Side Highway. No kiss, almost dead, and fully mortified. What a day. I wondered why I didn't feel worse. There was something so exhilarating about this whole experience, sore arm and hurt pride included. It was as if for the first time, I was fully engaged in life. The promise of a kiss, broken or not, and the threat of death, averted, had woken me up. I hated the sting of rejection, but at least I felt something.

FOLLOW YOUR DREAMS, EXCEPT THE ONE WHERE YOU'RE AT SCHOOL IN YOUR UNDERWEAR

⟋⟍

"WE NEED HELP. I'M CALLING STEVEN." John was a man on a mission. I could tell his adrenaline was still high from the chase, and he was silently concocting a plan to keep us safe. He got Steven on the phone immediately. "We are in New York. They found us outside of Grand Central Station. A cab-driver speaking Russian had orders to kill us, but not to recover the bag. I believe that the bag is worthless and that it's my charge they're after. We need a place to hide tonight." He was silent as he received his instructions. "Okay, we're headed there now. We'll head back to L.A. in the morning."

"SoHo Grand?" A girl could dream.

"PS 142, Brooklyn."

"What's that?"

"It's a middle school. It's Friday night, so it'll be locked up and empty for the weekend. We don't know what hotels they're watching, and we can't risk a big scene in a packed lobby, anyway. These guys won't mind blowing up a few hundred innocent people just to kill you. So I can't take you to an airport until we can rush directly on to a plane." His human side returned long enough for him to see the terror on my face. He put his arm around me and let it rest lightly on my shoulder. "Steven thinks we need to be someplace where there are no other people, just in case. Plus, it'll be like old times, camping out on the floor. I'll even let you pick . . . the gym or the science lab?"

"I can't remember the last time I slept on a real mattress. With clean sheets and a down pillow and maybe a bedside table with a cold glass of water and a book."

"Maybe there's a home ec class. We'll have the run of the place."

I smiled at him. He was trying to make me feel better, and I was not above letting him. "Do you mind if I get out of this costume?" He looked panicked. I went on, "Jeez, just look the other way, and I'm going to pull my jeans back on under this skirt. I'm not going to break into a middle school dressed like the principal."

John did as he was told, and I slipped back into my dirty but insanely comfortable jeans. I slipped out of my silk blouse and back into my T-shirt, careful to stay low enough not to register in the driver's rearview mirror and to hide the transfer of my phone. I powered it on in time to feel it vibrate with a few new texts. Would Olive give it a rest already?

"Okay, you can turn back." But John looked straight ahead, silent.

By the time the cab stopped in Brooklyn, I was sound asleep. John woke me up, paid the driver, and led me into a Chinese restaurant. He offered an apology in Chinese to the woman who tried to seat us and then asked her if we could leave through the back. We went out into the garbage-lined alley and followed it three blocks to the back door of PS 142. It was a large building, painted public school beige, with prison-style gates over the windows.

"Does every FBI agent have a key to PS 142?"

"Sort of." John pulled out his gun and fixed a silencer to the end. And as casually as if we were at the penny arcade, he shot off each of the four corners of the gate on the ground-floor window. He pulled off the gate and tossed it through the window (a less silent maneuver) and climbed through. "Come on in."

"You can't do that!" I stepped into what could have been a sixth grade classroom. Broken glass covered the floor, and the renegade security gate had knocked down a row of dioramas representing the polar biome. I was suddenly more afraid of the vice principal than the terrorists. "Are the kids going to show up for school on Monday and find their school vandalized? You know some kid's going to get blamed for this, that kid with the dirty hair and shifty eyes who just broods because no one will talk to him . . . They'll pin it on him, and it'll ruin his future . . ."

"Better than ending yours." We walked down the dark hallway and up a flight of stairs, looking for a windowless room where we could hide out in peace. We passed through the pitch-black main hallway, running our hands along a wall of lockers to guide us. We turned left at a small dark corridor, and John pushed open the first door on the right. He flipped on the lights to an office that must have belonged to the guidance counselor. "Now, how's this?" It was equipped with a long sofa, bean bag chairs, and a mini fridge—all the things that guidance counselors deem necessary to get kids to spill their guts.

I was beyond tired and starving. I headed for the fridge and found four juice boxes, a bottle of water, and a banana. I helped myself to all of it. Hell, we'd already committed major vandalism—why not add a little petty theft?

"I'm too tired to eat." John was taking the back cushions off the sofa to make more room.

"Where am I going to sleep? I can't lie down on a bean bag . . ." I was chugging juice boxes at this point and wiped my mouth with the back of my arm.

He lay down and patted the spot next to him. "There's plenty of room for both of us. Just imagine we have our air mattresses pushed together." These sound like mixed signals, right? But I'd been burned by false hope before, and frankly I was feeling a little too tired, scared, and hungry to pucker up, anyway.

I lay down, back to him, spoon style, and said, "This is fine."

"Good." He put his arm around me, not romantically but protectively, like he was afraid I might roll off the couch in my sleep. So I let myself fall asleep in his arms, heart rate normal and unaware of whether my breath stank or not. There was no romance forthcoming. There's such power in letting something go.

PANIC NOW

❧

THERE'S NOTHING WORSE THAN GETTING WOKEN up abruptly from a really good dream. Especially if you wake up in the arms of the world's dreamiest FBI agent with a gun in your face. I wish I were kidding.

I never heard them come in. I opened my eyes and couldn't figure out what I was looking at. It was metal and dark, and by the time I focused, I saw three men standing behind the one with the gun. I could feel John's arm tighten around me.

None of these guys looked like terrorists, which must be why I had a hard time getting my head around what was happening. They looked like a bunch of guys you'd see at the supermarket or at a movie. Their expressions weren't particularly menacing; they weren't wearing THINK GREEN T-shirts or carrying reusable bags. I could be wrong, but I think one of them might have been in a pair of Seven jeans.

The guy in charge had a long face and goatee and was speaking to John. "I'm not going to kill anyone in here. We're taking you outside. Leave your stuff."

John didn't move but held me even tighter. "She knows nothing. Take the diaper bag — that's what you need."

The guy to his left didn't seem to understand. "Why would we want the bag?" It was becoming obvious that the diaper bag theory was a figment of my imagination; they knew nothing about it. I'd set us out on a wild-goose chase to retrieve a bag full of nothing and was going to return home in a body bag full of me. Nice going, brainiac.

John let the diaper bag discussion go. "She can't hurt you; she can't identify anyone. I saw him. Let her go, and you can take me."

Longface said, "Get up." John stood up and put his arm securely around my waist. They frisked us both and took his gun, my last hope.

Longface reached out and took my face in his hands. He ran his fingers from my hairline, past my cheeks, and down to my neck. He rested his hands on my shoulders heavily and stared into my eyes with a hatred that I'd never seen before. And with as much hate, he smiled. I want to say that my blood ran cold with terror, but it was more like my blood stopped running at all. I was stone. All I could feel was the weight of John's hand still around my waist.

The boss finally spoke. "No, I think we'll do this my way. We're going to take you outside and kill you. And the girl, we'll take her with us. Won't that be fun?" He was smiling at me still, stroking my face. My mind raced through all the hideous things that were going to happen to me, and then settled on the hand on my waist. He was still here, I told myself. Who was I kidding?

Another one of the henchman approached John and placed a gun to his forehead. He grabbed him by the arm and dragged him away from me, toward the door. John looked back at me with a stare, as if he were trying to tell me something.

They marched us out of the office, barefoot, back down the long dark hallway. I walked behind Longface and in front of two others. John was to my right, followed by the guy who now had a gun to his back. It was dark in the hallway, but not so dark that I couldn't see John next to me staring straight ahead. I wondered how long until we got to where they would shoot him. I wondered how long they would keep me before they killed me too. I wondered what the rest of my life would have been like. Silently, I started to cry.

At the end of the hallway, we came to a set of double doors. The two guys behind me held them open for us and led us onto a walkway to what must have been a more modern addition to the school. It was a brick path lined with glass walls on either side that let the daylight stream in. The light burned my eyes at first, and I wondered what time it was. Looking down, I could see a track in the distance on one side and a baseball field on the other.

Out of nowhere I heard an explosive crash. My first thought was that I'd been shot, but I felt nothing but panic. The glass wall to my left had shattered and was raining tiny shards onto the grass below. While the glass was still falling, I was attacked from the back and propelled out the now-broken window. I landed behind a hedge with John flat on top of me and blood pouring from my arm. Without speaking, John pulled me to my feet and led me around the length of the hedge toward the back of the school. They had to be ten seconds behind us if they were going to jump, eighty seconds if they were going to take the stairs. John had one hand firmly around my good arm and a tiny gun that he must have had hidden (I don't even want to ask where, eeew!) in the other.

We raced silently around the perimeter of the school, our backs to the building. There was a house to the left of the school with a low fence that we could easily hop. I motioned to the plastic playhouse in the yard, a favorite childhood hiding place that might really come in handy now. John shook his head and mouthed: *Too dangerous*. Of course, John was still expecting a shootout and was trying to keep me away from innocent bystanders.

We backed around to the far side of the school and came to a fenced-in garden courtyard. I peered through the iron bars and could see a huge vegetable garden in its center, with rows of plants marked with handmade signs indicating what was growing there. Kale, spinach, Swiss chard. All the stuff middle school students like to eat. John tried the gate, but it was locked. Barbed wire topped the fence, presumably to keep kale-crazed kids from ravaging the garden, but now prohibiting us from climbing over to safety. As I walked along the fence, my right foot slipped into a hole and I fell to the ground. John motioned to me to *shhh*. (My hero. Not.) As I got up, I examined the muddy hole that I'd fallen into. A large hedgehog or raccoon must have dug under the fence for a snack. With a few more kicks of my bare foot, I carved out a space large enough to climb through. I motioned to John from the inside of the garden to climb under too. He dug it a little deeper and slid under. We repaired the hole with dirt from the tomato plants and silently walked to the only walled side of the garden. A large tarp lay on the ground next to the gardening equipment. We lay down and quickly pulled it up over us. We were either completely hidden or completely trapped, depending on how you look at it.

The silence was broken by the sound of steps on the wood chips surrounding the track. They were approaching the back of the school, moving toward the garden. John and I were completely still, pressed against the ground. My clothes were soaked from my muddy trip under the gate, and I was freezing. The stench that surrounded me suggested that the tarp over my face had been previously used either to transport fertilizer or as toilet paper. It was the least of my problems as I pressed my eyes shut and waited for the sound of gunfire. The footsteps were close now, and I heard the rattle of the iron gate. John reached a few inches over and grabbed my hand. We lay there like that for hours — okay, maybe a minute — until we heard their footsteps retreat back to the track.

We did not speak. After about ten minutes, John pulled me close to him and held me close. "It's okay," he whispered. I took this as my permission to start to sob. I had been minutes away from being tortured by terrorists; John had been that close to death. He was brushing my hair from my face. "It's okay now. Shhh. Let's just lay here for a few more minutes. Shhh. Where are you hurt?"

I stopped crying and used my good arm to wipe up my puddle of a face. After what he'd just done for me, I didn't need to torture John with my tears. "I think I landed on a sprinkler head or a rock or something. My arm is cut, same arm I landed on when you threw me out of the cab. What's with you and tossing me into harm's way? Some bodyguard."

He laughed and hugged me again. "Let's wait here for a little bit, just to be sure they are gone. Then we'll get out of here and get somewhere safe. I'll take care of your arm."

As safe as this? I couldn't wait to see Plan B. "Where are we going now?"

He lifted the tarp a little to let some air in. "You'll see when we get there; it's hard to explain."

At this point I owed my life to John, so there was nothing I could do but trust that he was going to do everything he could to keep me safe. I was probably in shock but knew enough to take full advantage of the fact that he was still holding me and stroking my hair. I looked up at him, and we were nose to nose. "Would you really have gone with them in my place?"

"Yes. My first choice was to get us both out of there. But if someone was going to die, it was going to be me." He looked away, as if embarrassed by his own chivalry. "I mean, it's my job."

"Right. Well, thanks." I turned away from him and lay on my back. I was stiff on the cold, hard brick, listening for footsteps, and wishing I was wearing socks . . . when it hit me. "What about our stuff?"

"What, our FBI-issued toothbrushes? And that sinister diaper bag that no one seems to want?"

"I was thinking more about my boots." I looked over at him hopefully, willing him to agree to go back into the school without making me explain why I loved those boots so much.

He laughed at me. "What if we just try to live through the rest of the day, and then I'll buy you a new pair of boots?"

"Thanks but no thanks. They can't be replaced."

"What? Do they have special powers or something?"

"Maybe. Plus, we should get the diaper bag. It may mean nothing, but I'd like to have a closer look at those numbers."

He ran his hands along his pockets. "I actually think I left my phone in there too. Okay, I'll go, but I'm leaving you right here. They could have gone back into the building. I can't risk having you with me."

But I can't stand being away from you. Oh, thank God I didn't say it out loud. "Never mind, it's not worth it. We can get to your next safe spot without shoes. And maybe we can call the school on Monday to get the diaper bag and your phone back."

"That might require a little more explaining than I want to do. I'll go. Promise me you won't move. Promise."

"Promise."

He pulled his arm out from under me and hesitated like he was going to say something. "What?" I asked.

"Nothing. I'll be right back. Now, seriously, don't move. If I go in there for your boots and come back to find your feet gone, I'm going to be pissed."

I smiled at his attempt at levity. "Okay, thanks." He got up and disappeared behind the kale. It was maybe ten in the morning from the way the light looked. I pulled the tarp up over my head and willed time to speed up. I imagined his every step. He's gone back under the fence; he's walked the perimeter of the school; he's climbed through the broken window. He's gone down the hall and up the stairs; he's grabbed the bags; he's making his way back out. Gunshot. I heard a muffled shot—I was sure of it. It was just one, but it was enough.

I was too panicked to cry. I was lying in John's arms ten minutes before, ready to get up and go to a safe place, but I'd sent him back in for my boots. And some papers. They were probably coming for me now, and I didn't even care. I'd just killed him, after everything he'd risked for me. I just lay there like stone in total disbelief, even as I heard the footsteps. Even as they got closer, I didn't really care. I just stared up at the dark tarp over me and waited for the next gunshot.

The tarp was pulled off of me, all in one motion. I squinted against the sunlight and saw him smiling, holding our bags in one hand and my boots in the other. "What's wrong with you?"

I sat up and pulled my knees to my forehead. "Are you kidding me? What was that gunshot?"

He knelt down next to me. "Oh, I'm sorry. I didn't think about you hearing that. I just didn't want to climb back out the broken window, so I shot the lock on the gym door."

"Oh." I reached for my boots but winced at the pain of straightening my bloody arm.

"Let me help you with those." He took my left boot and started to help me put it on, Prince Charming style, when my phone slid out of the boot onto the tarp. We both stared at it lying there, guilty like a dirty magazine or a bloody knife. He picked it up, shaking his head. "Who's Olive Grossman and why is she asking if Danny would look good in a white tux? You told me you didn't have a phone."

"Olive's taking Danny to the Senior Prom?!"

"This isn't *Gossip Girl*, Farrah. This phone could be what nearly got us killed. Ever heard of the Find My iPhone app? It can track your phone to within a three-yard radius." He was pacing and furiously trying to spring my SIM card out with the tip of his pen. "Jonas Furnis could easily have someone working at AT&T. Or Verizon. Or wherever. You lied to me."

"It's not like I've been texting back. I mean, I'm supposed to be kidnapped and everything . . ."

"That makes no difference." He gave up on my SIM card and threw the whole phone on the ground, shattering the screen instantly. He stomped on it full force with the heel of his shoe, just for good measure, and kicked the pieces into the tomato plants. "And let's just not talk for a little while, okay?"

In silence, we dug our way out of the garden and made our way back down the alley, past the Chinese restaurant, to the subway.

MY OTHER CAR IS A LIMO

WHEN WE GOT OUT OF THE subway at Seventy-ninth Street, it was noon. I was a little shaken, and my arm was bleeding pretty badly. We got up to the top of the stairs at street level and looked both ways up and down Lexington Avenue. It was business as usual here. People were rushing to the park or to lunch or home to sleep after a big night out. That may be the most exciting thing about New York—the fact that everyone there is doing something totally different. A woman with a $15,000 handbag waited at the light next to a Vietnamese delivery guy on a bike. The richness of it was not lost on me, even at that moment.

John stopped and pulled out his pocketknife from his backpack and sliced off the tails of his button-down shirt. He quickly bandaged my arm with it.

"Too tight," I complained.

"Too bad," he replied, putting his arm around me and leading me down Seventy-ninth Street. I wondered how such a beautiful city could be so dirty. And I wondered if we were the dirtiest people in the city. It had been exactly eight days since my last hot shower and nine days since I last shaved my legs. Unfortunately, I'm not one of those girls who just gets the tiniest bit of downy blond fuzz on her lower legs. I'm more like one of those girls who gets a five o'clock shadow on her legs by noon. My need for a razor was becoming a national emergency.

Also, I was starving and cold. I could tell John was still pissed, but his arm was around me and I leaned my head over onto his shoulder as we walked. I was injured, so I could get away with this sort of thing. I was enjoying the sounds of the city, the traffic, the horns, and the shouting. I didn't want to interrupt it by asking John exactly where we'd be staying. Correction: spending the night.

Just before we got to the end of the long block separating Lexington Avenue from Park Avenue, John steered me into an alleyway. We were wedged between a dry cleaner and a townhouse with a spilled garbage can blocking any further access. John helped me over the garbage can and carefully placed his hands on my shoulders. Gently, he pushed me up against the brick wall of the townhouse. He stood with his chest against mine, his lips at my forehead, and his hands against the wall. I could see his breath as his mouth got closer to mine. I didn't know where the change of heart was coming from, but, well, it was about time. Sometimes all you need is a near-death experience.

I looked up at him to make the kiss unavoidable. I think in my head I'd already been kissing him since we got off the subway; it was time for him to catch up. But when I looked up, I saw that he wasn't looking at me at all. He was focused intently on the brick to the left of my ear. Great. I meet the perfect guy, and he's too shy to kiss me.

"John, it's okay . . ." I said, encouragingly.

"It . . . is . . . almost . . . okay . . . got it." I looked over my shoulder at the brick and saw that it was an electronic keypad with a thumbprint reader. Very cool, but where the hell was my kiss? The light flashed green, then flashed faster, until three beeps were followed by a cracking sound.

The exact spot where we were standing moved beneath us and, still leaning against the wall, we were shifted into the building. I couldn't tell where we were, but it felt like we were in a tiny elevator that was meant only to hold one person.

John was holding me tight to make room for the door to close. I'm not normally boy crazy — you should know that about me by now. But this was getting ridiculous. I had no clue where we were, and frankly I did not much care. I looked up at him and touched his face.

More with the talking: "Don't you want to know where we are?"

I wasn't about to let go of the face; smelling and touching his skin at the same time was making me a bit dizzy. "Are we where we are spending the night?"

"No, we're where we're staying."

I snapped to reality. "Staying? Do you mean staying? Clean sheets? Minibar?"

"Something like that." And with that the elevator door opened, and we were there. Where we were staying. The first thing I felt was a gust of warm air. Heat! The entrance (or is it a foyer?) was paneled in a light oak with a black and red Oriental rug and an antique table with a statue of some armless goddess that I couldn't identify. What I could identify was an original Degas oil painting that I'd studied in school. Where were we?

"You bring a lot of girls here?"

"Just you. I figure you're over the wall. Plus I am getting sick of sleeping on an air mattress and wasn't looking forward to showering in a gas station sink tonight."

Over the wall? Maybe. Over the moon? For sure.

"So you happened to find a magic brick that allows us to break into someone's townhouse? I'm all for the fancy digs, but aren't we in enough trouble already?"

A loud gong interrupted me. *Great,* I thought, *here comes the security company, and there goes my night in clean sheets.*

John walked into a small den and reached for a phone attached to the mirrored wall of the wet bar. "William? Yeah, hey, it's me. I know, sorry, they didn't know I'd be here either. Uh-huh, I'm just in town for a few days. No, I don't need anything. Well, yeah, I guess. Hang on." He put his hand over the phone and turned to see me with my mouth hanging open. "Are you more of a steak person or a seafood person?"

"Steak?"

"Okay, a couple of steaks and those good fries you do would be great. Maybe a couple of Coronas, for medicinal purposes." I got a wink. "And some Cokes and maybe a little . . . hang on. Are you more of a chocolate person or a cheesecake person?"

"Chocolate?" I barely got it out.

"Chocolate cake? Great, thanks so much. No rush. Oh, and I need six large bandages and some rubbing alcohol. And maybe a razor? Okay, bye."

I wanted to say, "Make that two razors. Stat." But I couldn't get it out fast enough. I plopped down on the den's deep chestnut leather sofa and asked the obvious question: "Where are we?"

John smiled the half smile and picked up a framed photo from over the bar. He handed it to me, and I immediately recognized a ten-year-old John with a young couple who must have been his parents. They were seated under a thatched umbrella at a table overlooking the ocean, maybe the Mediterranean Sea.

"My parents both work for the CIA. That's why we moved around so much when I was growing up. And every few years, things would get too hot in the Middle East or someone would start to suspect them of spy stuff in Europe, and we'd have to go into hiding. So this is our hideout. No one ever sees us walk in or out of the front door. Our neighbors think William lives here alone, which he does most of the time, but he's really our butler."

So this was his house? I spotted the expensive suit on day one, but I never would have taken him for a Manhattan townhouse-owning art collector. "Where are your parents now?"

"I never know. I can't. There's a lot of baggage between the FBI and the CIA, and everyone's listening to everyone all the time. So they call me when they're between gigs, and I go meet them for a long weekend in Mexico or Costa Rica or somewhere. We are always here for Christmas. No one knows about this place — not the CIA, not the FBI, nobody."

I walked around the den, shamelessly picking up photos and examining them for more information. The photos all seemed normal enough but not. John was six years old with his soccer team, but they were in Tanzania. John was riding a bike, maybe for the first time, but the street is cobblestone. The Christmas photos were all taken in this house, around the fire with stockings and a tree and the works. They seemed as happy and normal as my family, not caring at all that they were hiding out.

John had moved into the living room and was making a fire. I plopped onto the huge brown velvet sofa, kicked off my boots, and surveyed the grandeur. Everything was beautiful but nothing was frilly. Everything went together but nothing matched. The room did not look like something from a magazine, where a gifted designer had assembled beautiful fabrics and rugs to create a particular feeling. This room was decidedly less deliberate, where everything seemed to have meaning and a history. The room, like the family itself, was a collection of countries and experiences. An antique French chair had a handmade African blanket tossed on the back. An asymmetrical crystal bowl from the Czech Republic dwarfed the coffee table. This room quietly told the story of John's family, of where they'd been and what they'd chosen to take with them. It was a little like my bedroom, where the bumper stickers told the story of who I was becoming. Okay, it may be as personal as my room, but the similarities ended there. This room said: *Yeah, this all cost a bundle, but feel free to sit anywhere, put your drink down, and enjoy.* I planned to do just that.

Dinner came up through a dumbwaiter. "Just like old times," John said as he pulled out our steaks on china dishes, our Cokes in crystal glasses, a silver bucket filled with Coronas, and perfectly ironed linen napkins.

"Not exactly."

"Listen, promise me you're not going to pull anything like that cell phone stunt again. People who are famous for killing people are trying to kill us. And that could have been how they found us. We have to be totally honest with each other, deal?" I nodded. "Let me take care of your arm." John sat down next to me in front of the fire. He untied his shirt-tail bandage and revealed a fairly nasty cut. I looked away, but he was unfazed. He took some rubbing alcohol and started to clean it. I winced because it hurt like hell. John kept talking to me in a doctor's voice. "That's it, just one more second . . . Let me dry it up and then — there you go — all bandaged. Are you okay?" He was so close to me that it hurt a little. I looked down to avoid his eyes, knowing that if he saw how I was feeling, I'd have to endure another I-don't-like-you-that-way speech. I wasn't going down that road again.

I scooted over to the coffee table covered with food. We ate in silence, occasionally looking up at each other to smile at our good fortune. We were both starving and tired and happy to be temporarily warm and safe. I slowed down a little when I got halfway through my steak. "So who were your friends growing up?"

"No one, really. I made friends wherever we stayed, but then we'd move and I couldn't exactly leave a forwarding address. When we lived in France, I was Mark; when we were in Iran, I was Dominic. I spent a lot of time mastering how not to be myself, so my friendships were pretty superficial. I mean not being able to be honest with anyone and not being able to let them know you at all — it's a pretty weird way to grow up."

"Tell me about it." I laughed. "Did it ever get better?"

"I decided to go to boarding school in Connecticut at thirteen, and my parents were happy that I would have a more normal life. They came for parents' weekend when they could, and I'd spend summers in Martha's Vineyard with my aunt and her kids or at our house in Connecticut."

"You have another bat cave in Connecticut?"

"No, that house is actually public knowledge. It's our official address. But it's very carefully designed not to reveal too much about us. Everything in it was chosen by a decorator, and my mom hates it. This place is more personal."

And personal it was. John was still the same guy I'd been in captivity with, but seeing him against this backdrop opened him up. It added a dimension to him that was a bit deeper and explained why he was so unavailable. I could tell he was still a little hesitant to have me here.

"Did you make friends in boarding school?" I was dipping my last French fry in a tiny crystal bowl of ketchup.

"Yes and no. I was a little out of it socially because I'd spent so little time in the States. I knew nothing about the music they were listening to or the TV shows they were watching. I'd smuggle all the teen magazines I could find into my room and study them for all the popular culture I'd missed. I got pretty good at smiling and nodding like I knew what people were talking about." He was laughing a little as he remembered. "Typical oddball teenager trying to fit in. It was sort of pathetic."

"Been there." I was trying to take small bites of my cake to make it last.

"What? You're so . . . well, except for the . . . Yeah, that must be kind of weird."

"It's a little more than weird. In middle school I was a total outcast. They called me Digit."

John laughed a little longer than I thought was polite. "Digit? It's so perfect for you. So much better than Farrah."

"Yeah, thanks. My brother thinks the same thing. He hasn't called me Farrah since I was eleven. I've been a dork since I was little; he thinks I should just embrace it."

"*De pequenino se torce o pepino.* The Portuguese say: 'From very small the cucumber is bent.' When you're born, you are already shaped, nerd or not."

"'Bent' is probably a pretty good way to describe me." I

was wiping the last crumbs of chocolate cake off of my plate with my finger and suddenly felt really vulnerable. If I was so crazy about this guy, why was I telling him what a loser I am? "Did you like learning a new language every year, or was it just survival?"

"I loved it. Languages come really easily to me, obviously, but more than that I felt like really understanding a language helped me to understand the people there. It was like something I could hold on to when I left. Just listening to their idioms tells you so much about what they value. Most cultures have idioms that are based in nature, like the cucumber thing, to describe the human experience. Like we are no different from the soil and the trees. It's kind of like your thing with numbers, looking into a big messy language to find some logical link to our roots. I find it kind of relaxing." He looked away like he thought maybe he'd said too much.

I smiled at him. "When I was little, I used to have these anxiety attacks when I'd come across an uneven brick path or a group of numbers that had no connection at all. My mom would have me lie down and imagine a forest that seemed to be in complete chaos. She'd describe the noise and the smell and the mess and the constant action. And then she'd start to uncover the logic, how the gorillas eat the seeds and fertilize the soil so that new trees can grow and provide homes for the birds, how the bugs work the soil and provide food for the birds . . . She'd talk for a long time until I could see the forest working as an organism in complete order. Unfortunately, as I got older, I couldn't bring my mom everywhere I went. So I went to see a hypnotherapist a few years ago who helped me do pretty much the same thing, just by looking at a tree . . . when I need to, I mean. Which isn't as often as it used to be."

John was nodding at me like he totally understood that. What kind of a person wouldn't think that was crazy? "I guess the idea is that when things seem crazy, it's just because you're not seeing the bigger picture."

"Exactly. Which is how I try to think about high school.

It's like my whole life now, but maybe it's just a small part of the whole story. And high school has been better, anyway. I've kept the whole genius thing on the down low, and I have friends. Even if they have no clue who I am."

"You'll like college. It's just a bigger, better selection of people, and no one's really in it to conform." John shrugged and reached across the table to take my plate. "Think of it this way: at least we're not those people who peaked in high school and sleep next to their prom photos."

"So college was more normal for you?" I asked, hopefully. If his story was as much like mine as I'd imagined, I'd like to know it had a happy ending.

"It could have been. I met a lot of people at Princeton that I could relate to, people from all over the world with different life experiences. But I was really focused on graduating in two and a half years, so I didn't really socialize that much."

"What's with you and the big rush?" I asked, reaching for a beer as a dessert after dessert. I wondered if I would ever be full again.

He got up to stoke the fire, which in no way needed stoking, and carefully avoided my eye. "My dad asks the same question all the time. He thinks it's ridiculous, but I've always been set on getting this one job in the FBI. It's highly selective, and they often pick young people who show the propensity to achieve quickly and beyond their years. It's called Special Sector."

"Sounds special." I think maybe I was with his dad— where's the fire?

John seemed to either not get or not care that I was making fun of him. "Most people don't know about it, but its members have the highest level of security clearance in the FBI and are privy to the most critical operations happening in the U.S. at any given time. My dad had the chance at Special Sector and turned it down. I can't imagine." He let out a big breath, like he'd just gotten something off his chest.

"So that's your big goal? Then what?" I finished the last

three bites of his cake and leaned back into the huge sofa behind me.

"I guess a long career in the FBI. Maybe I'll run it someday." John offered a fake laugh and shrugged a little, as if he
was a little embarrassed by having shared his long-term plan.
"It's a long shot. They only take one new guy every few years.
Let's just see if we can make it through this week alive."

ROMANCE IS LIKE A GAME OF CHESS: ONE FALSE MOVE AND YOU'RE MATED

ᘐ

"DOES THIS MANSION OF YOURS HAVE a shower?" I was seriously getting used to the Four Seasons treatment.

"Sure, you can use my parents' shower. Rifle around in my mom's closet for some pajamas. Between the bathroom and the closets, there's another dumbwaiter. Press the black button, throw your dirty stuff in, and then press the red button to send it down."

He gestured to a flight of stairs that led to what must have been the third floor. I climbed them obediently and looked down to the far end of the hall to a closed door. The promise of a hot shower and really nice towels drew me down that hall like I was dying and moving toward the light. I opened the door and realized I'd been right. This was heaven. His parents' room had a regal flair to it. There was a huge king-size four-poster bed with crisp white linens. Beyond it was a wall of French doors, flanked by white linen curtains, that looked out over Park Avenue and at Central Park's treetops in the distance. I opened the doors, the breeze blowing the curtains into the room. The view was like a spa for my mind. Central Park is a perfectly shaped giant rectangle, and from a distance all the trees appear to be the exact same height. The kidney shaped reservoir is slightly off center but is balanced by kidney-shaped meadows dotted by baseball diamonds. The park is lined by buildings on every side, and as I looked across to the far side of the park, I could see the setting sun shining on a silver line of buildings, making a sharp edge to the park's border. Central Park had to be home to thousands of species of trees, but from this height, I couldn't tell an elm from an oak. It was just an orderly mass of green, all living peacefully together. *This should be the photo I keep in my phone for emergencies,* I thought.

On Park Avenue, the city raced past me in both directions. Yellow taxis, black Town Cars, garbage trucks, and Mercedes sedans constantly changed lanes to jockey for position. I imagined a video game where all these different players were swerving in and out of traffic, trying to knock down the bicycle messengers. A woman crossed the street below, beautifully dressed in what appeared to be a beige cashmere blazer, gray pants, and six-inch heels. She walked as surely as if she were in sneakers, head up and fully confident that no unanticipated pothole would take her down. I wanted to be that woman. I wanted to move through the world with my head up. How many times had I almost been killed this week? I was running out of things to be afraid of. *Potholes,* I thought, *bring it on.*

Their bathroom was dark pink marble with a glass box in the corner that I assumed was the shower. I took off my sticky, smelly, bloody clothes and turned on the hot water. I slowly peeled off the dressing on my arm, grateful that the bleeding had stopped. Obediently, I put all my stuff in the dumbwaiter, half worried I'd never see it again.

The showerhead came directly from the ceiling and let out a hard stream of water that had to be a foot in diameter. And because heaven is a place where no needs are unmet, the small shelf with shampoo, conditioner, and gardenia soap also had a razor. I let the water run as hot as I could stand it and just stood there, feeling every inch of my body become clean.

I felt changed somehow as that water ran down my back. Maybe it was coming so close to death that made me feel alive, almost invigorated. I hadn't slept for more than a few hours in a row since the night before the attack on JFK, and my body ached from exhaustion. But mentally I felt like I wasn't working as hard as I usually was, like it was a welcome break to quit dragging around a fake identity. Plus there was a slight current of energy running through me, just from being with John. I told myself that I didn't care that much that my feelings were unrequited and that I would definitely end up hurt. Hell, I could also end up dead. What mattered was this feeling of letting someone know me and having him let me in too. Any awkwardness between us had disappeared completely, as if there was no longer any reason to pause to think before speaking. Bottom line: It felt easier to be with John than it had ever felt being without him.

I toweled off and headed into what had to be Mrs. Bennett's dressing room. I cringed at what an incredible invasion of privacy this was, looking through her things while wrapped in her towel. I could tell she wasn't a fussy person. Her dressing table had a mirror, a brush, moisturizer, a lipstick, and a poorly fashioned clay lion with the initials JB carved underneath. That's it. Her closet had mahogany shelves on the left and hanging racks on the right. The drawers at the end suggested unmentionables, and I wasn't that desperate. I had sent mine down in the dumbwaiter. Her shelves sported all shades of earth tones and all grades of cashmere. I only found one pair of pajamas but quickly put them back in search of something a little scruffier. I thumbed through stacks of beautiful shirts and scarves and beach cover-ups. But the stained cotton oversize nightshirt I searched for was woefully absent. So I went back to her only pair of pajamas and carefully unfolded them: ivory silk with little pearl buttons, professionally ironed. Were these people for real?

I found my way back down to the living room in bare feet, feeling a little nervous both because I was in John's mother's pajamas and because they were so beautiful that I thought it looked like I was trying too hard. John was nowhere to be found, so I roamed around tentatively, already worried that I was sweating or ruining the perfect crease in the pants.

"Digit? I'm up here." John was calling from upstairs on the fourth floor. I walked up the red carpeted stairs and found a hallway identical to the one to his parents' room but with an open door at the end. "I'm in my room," he was calling. I took the smallest steps down the hallway, feeling nervous and pretty and suddenly so awkward. I needed my uniform back, at least my boots. I walked in and gave him what I am sure was the smile of a four-year-old looking for approval after poorly coloring in an outline of Elmo.

John was sitting up in bed, dressed in a Princeton T-shirt and boxers. His face fell when he saw me, moving from a welcoming smile to a pained grimace. "Hi."

"Hey. I found these in your mom's room; they were the only ones there. Should I have just put my stuff back on? I put it all in the dumbwaiter and pressed the red button like you said, but I guess I could press the black one and get it back and then just put it on. It was red to send it down, right? What's the matter?"

"Nothing. It's just you. Well, you and the way you look in my mother's pajamas. It's just a little freaky, and I think I'm going to need therapy for a long time."

I relaxed with the whiff of approval. "Can I go outside?" John's room was identical in format to his parents, with a slightly smaller sleigh bed and the balcony beyond it with a higher view of Park Avenue and the Central Park treetops.

"Sure." John hurried to join me outside, and we stood there, both in our PJs, looking out on the city as if we were completely alone. That was the quality of New York that I felt earlier as we raced from the subway, this idea that you are so completely surrounded by people that you are really all alone. At this moment, I loved it.

"New York is the perfect place for a family like yours."

John knew exactly what I meant. "The best food in the

world and not a single one of our neighbors cares who we are. It's worked for us for a long time. I'm really glad you're here, Digit."

"Are you going to keep calling me that?"

"Probably—it's perfect. There's a reason it stuck. Does it bother you?"

I thought for a second and answered honestly, "For some reason, no."

A cool wind blew past us, and John put his arm around me. "Let's get you inside."

We went in but left the French doors open. John started walking toward the hallway, and I climbed into bed. "Hang on. This is my room. I'll walk you down to my parents' room, come on."

I put my head down and pulled the heavy down comforter up to my chin. "No."

"Come on. We're sleeping on our own tonight. There's no need to . . ."

"No." I was not getting out of that bed for anything.

"Okay, Digit. I'll admit it." He sat down on the side of the bed next to me. "I feel something too. A lot of something. But it's got to be wrong. You're seventeen years old. I am responsible for you, and if I give in now, who does that make me?"

I was so tired all of a sudden, I think even some of my hormones were starting to fall asleep. Without lifting my head, I said, "John, I feel a lot of things that I don't have the energy to express right now, and I don't think I've been exactly stealth about concealing them. But at this moment I'm feeling the effects of being thrown from a moving car, held at gunpoint, and tossed through a plate-glass window. You, incredibly attractive or not, might be the only thing that stands between my waking up in the morning and my being chopped up in my sleep. I am staying here, and so are you. And these fine silk pajamas are staying on. Now get in bed."

He had no response to that. He walked around to the other side of the bed and climbed in. I was so comfortable and so safe in that bed. I stretched out and turned to take one last look at John before I went to sleep, but he was a step ahead of me. He was lying on his side, propped up on his elbow, looking at me in the oddest way. "What?"

"You know, for the longest time I have been so focused on the future. I've had a list of things I've wanted to accomplish since I was old enough to make a list. I am smack in the middle of the biggest challenge of my career so far, the outcome of which will determine my future, dead or alive—a success or a failure. Tonight when I was telling you about it all, I realized that right now, for the first time in my life, I only really want two things." He touched my neck and looked at me so earnestly. "I just want to get you out of this. And then I want you to turn eighteen."

With his hand still on my neck, he leaned down and kissed me. It was exactly like a kiss in a dream: a slow, soft kiss, not nearly long enough but long enough for it to matter. Of course, it was John who finally pulled away.

"Sorry," he said, kissing me lightly once more and brushing my hair from my face. I'd never seen a less sorry person in my life.

"I forgive you," I said. And I went to sleep.

HONK IF YOU LOVE PEACE AND QUIET

WHEN I WOKE UP IN THE morning, I realized where I was before I opened my eyes. I wanted to remember it perfectly in case my parents didn't want me to make a habit of shacking up with older guys on a school night. The first thing I felt was his skin on my back, warm and asleep. Then the smell of him, his own smell like clean skin combined with the smell of that great gardenia soap I'd used.

I turned to look at him while he slept. I had the rare opportunity to stare, to take him in without his knowing. His closed eyes seemed wider than usual, and his expressionless face seemed younger. Asleep, he was not the know-it-all trying to do the job of a man ten years older. Asleep, he was a kid like me. His ears were nondescript, which I think is the best way for ears to be. But on his left ear was the faintest mark of a long ago closed-up piercing, maybe an act of preteen rebellion while living in Prague.

I wondered what he would be like when he woke up. Was last night a post-traumatic we-almost-got-killed-so-we-might-as-well-make-out-a-little situation? Was he going to phone into the FBI and confess and then caution me against ever coming near him again, lest I compromise his chances at Special Whatever? I had my answer almost immediately.

He started to wake up. I felt like I was about to be caught rifling through his underwear drawer, so I quickly closed my eyes and pretended that I had not just spent fifteen minutes memorizing the layout of his DNA. He brushed his lips softly over mine. "Hey, Digit. You still seventeen?"

"I can't remember."

"Me either," he said. Then he kissed me, and it struck me that not only was he the best, most fantastic kisser in the world, but that he was the only person I have ever known or heard of who does not have morning breath. The world's only completely delicious person.

This went on for a long time, or not. It's really hard to say. I was living in this time-space continuum that existed only in the one-inch perimeter around John's body, in a world that was only that bed. When he spoke, even the sound of his voice surprised me. "Are you okay with this?"

"What do you think?" I said, kissing him again.

"I just want to make sure. This doesn't seem like the kind of thing I can backtrack on. I mean, I'm not going to be able to go back to being your buddy and guardian."

"Then don't." This was all so clear to me. I couldn't understand what the big deal was. But what did I know? After all, I was the minor who was already plotting how to get him to turn this misdemeanor into a felony.

"Okay. So this is okay?"

I laughed at him a little. There's no way I seemed like I was under duress. "Yes, this is okay." I rolled over on top of him, just to make my point. "I'm pretty sure it was okay a week ago, but it's definitely okay now. But just to make sure, let's take the day off from running from the bad guys." I was honestly in such a fog that I didn't know how I was going to function outside of that bed.

John pulled the covers up to our shoulders. "That's all I want to do. They'll never find us under here," he said.

The switch in my brain flipped to warm-up mode, but I kissed him anyway. The slightest spark of actual mental activity was making its way through the stupor I'd slipped into. I kissed him again, but the thought started to take form, despite my best efforts.

"What's wrong?" John was kissing my neck and making it nearly impossible to answer the question.

"It couldn't have been my phone they were tracking. They would have found us back in the warehouse. So it's strange that they have found us at Grand Central Station and at the school, but they haven't found us here."

Yawn. His switch was still firmly in the off position. "That's because no one knows this place exists." He kissed me again and, as much as I wanted to keep that going for the next six to twelve hours, my mind would not shut up.

I sat up. "But no one has ever known where we were, except for Steven. But we keep getting found. And the one time you don't check in, we haven't been found."

Flick. I think I see a connection. John swung his legs over the side of the bed and ran his fingers through his now getting-a-little-long-in-the-dreamiest-possible-way hair. "You think *my* phone is tapped?"

"Or maybe there's someone inside the FBI who's selling us out. Someone close to Steven, someone in your group."

John switched fully to FBI mode and pulled a pair of jeans out of his dresser. He started walking downstairs. Sorry I'd brought it up, I got out of bed and followed him. John ordered eggs Benedict, waffles with raspberries and whipped cream, four croissants, coffee, and orange juice for breakfast.

We sat down on the terrace to eat, and I broke the silence. "I think I know how to find out. It's pretty simple first-season *Law and Order*." And then I heard it: *creak* as the secret elevator opened, and *slam* as the steel door closed behind an intruder. John jumped out of his seat and shoved me behind a topiary. He had his gun in his hand in an instant. Funny what you think when you are in mortal danger. I did not see my life pass before my eyes. I just wondered what kind of person eats waffles with a concealed weapon in ready position.

The terrace door was open, and we could hear them looking around the apartment. They were opening and closing doors, and I could hear their steps getting closer.

When they finally appeared on the terrace, my confusion mounted. There were two of them, they seemed to be un- armed, and they were beautifully dressed.

"God." John gasped, relieved. "Hi, Mom. Hi, Dad." He put his gun away and walked over to hug them. "What are you doing here?"

John's mother was tall and serious. She had that polished but no-nonsense look that French women have, suggesting that they'd been born beautiful and had to exert very little ef- fort to stay that way. "Johnny, we could not get in touch with you through the L.A. Bureau and finally heard you were away on assignment. But this morning we got a call from William saying that you had arrived here last night injured. Of course, we had to come. Are you all right?"

Okay, here's a way to make a good first impression. Don't get up—just stay crouched behind the topiary as if you are still expecting gunshots. John started to explain that it had actually been me who was hurt and gestured to where I should have been standing, casually next to him, fully dressed and ready to make an awesome first impression. When I wasn't there, he spotted me—Crouching Tiger, Hidden Idiot—and reached out his hand to help me up.

"Mom, Dad, this is Farrah Higgins." I managed to stand all the way up, brushed the potting soil off my hands, and said hello. "Farrah, these are my parents, Henry and Margaret Bennett." I had the feeling they were not the sort of people I'd be calling Hank and Marge after the wedding.

"Hello, dear," the missus said quickly, eyeing her now-wrinkled pajamas and then turning back to John. "So you are here with a young woman?"

"How old are you, young lady?" asked his father.

"Seventeen," I managed.

Proving that no matter how chic and worldly, all moms are alike, John's mom leaned in to him and said, "Darling, this is hardly appropriate, such a young girl and unchaperoned, and while you are supposed to be on a case . . ."

"Mom, stop. It's nothing like that! This *is* my case. Farrah has cracked a major terror plot, and I am hiding her while we get to the bottom of it."

Nothing like *that*? I thought it was starting to be something like *that*. It really felt like it was exactly *that*. Maybe I'm underage and this is a major misdemeanor, but come on! Own up!

So I stood there feeling like a stray cat that Johnny Freakin' Do-Gooder was hired to escort home. "I am the love of his life, actually. We just spent the last twelve hours snuggled up in your Egyptian cotton sheets. I even used your razor! So if you think I am some charity case the FBI has picked up, you are sadly mistaken." So that's what I felt like saying. But instead I said, "We have made a lot progress on the case." Lame, I know.

Mrs. Bennett looked relieved, as if she was making a mental list: Son not a pedophile — check.

John was acting maddeningly casual, like his parents were always walking in, unannounced, to his love nest. "Should I have William send up some more coffee? Can you guys join us for breakfast?"

John's parents exchanged a glance, and Mr. Bennett said, "Just for a minute. I'll have coffee and blueberry pancakes. Your mother will have the same but make her pancakes whole wheat." What I wouldn't give to see that magic kitchen.

We all sat down on the terrace, looking out over the tops of other Park Avenue buildings. In the distance, the perfect tree line of Central Park calmed my nerves a little.

Mr. Bennett was a man of few words, but I could tell he was well schooled in the spy business. He seemed to take in every detail around him without moving his head more than five degrees in either direction. I saw him notice how close together John's and my chairs were at the table, and the way John had to move his to even out the foursome when we all sat down. He was on to us, and his mental checklist was reading: Son is a pedophile — check.

He started quizzing us. "Farrah, how did you get hurt?"

"We were hiding out in a middle school Friday night. It was locked up for the weekend, so we were sure we were safe—"

John jumped in. "But we weren't obviously. Four guys got in and held us at gunpoint and nearly marched us to our deaths—"

"Until John had the bright idea that we jump, me first!" I was laughing and so was he.

"Lucky for me, Farrah broke my fall . . ."

"And protected him from the sprinkler that was sticking up from the grass below. I cut my arm, the same arm I bruised earlier when John dragged me out of a moving taxi . . ."

"She's heavier than she looks," he teased.

"Hey." I smacked him in the arm playfully. I looked over at the Bennetts and realized that we had totally blown it. We were being way too cute. John looked up and saw it too. His mother had her arms crossed, and her eyebrows were threatening her hairline. His dad had a faint smile on his face, slightly amused.

We both recovered and straightened ourselves up. John started talking a mile a minute, and I started shoving croissants into my mouth. It seemed like the only way to keep me from speaking. And it was clear that, as long as I was within two feet of John Bennett, if I was speaking, I was gushing.

Mrs. Bennett scolded John. "You were crazy to go hide out in a school when you could have been completely safe here. Why would you have gone there?"

Wait. That was a good point. John looked down as he spoke. "I just wanted to do this on my own. I wanted to successfully complete my first field assignment without leaning on you guys." He glanced at me. "And I nearly got her killed."

"But you didn't," Mr. Bennett offered. "Now, what is this case about? Who wants to kill Farrah?"

John explained, "I can't give you all the details of this case, of course, but Farrah and I are starting to think that we have been compromised in some way. We are being found in normally secure locations, when no one has been informed about our whereabouts except for my team at the FBI. It's possible that my cell phone is tapped or that there is a leak from within the Bureau. We were safe last night, but it was the one night that I did not call the office to check in."

"That's not like you, John. Why wouldn't you have reported in?" His mother's eyebrows were now reaching an unprecedented latitude.

"We were really tired, and Farrah was hurt, and, well, I forgot."

Mr. Bennett jumped in to save his son. "It sounds like you're right—you may be compromised in some way. And it may be key to your investigation to determine who is sympathizing with the criminals. I don't think you have any option other than to set up a sting and try to catch them."

"I was thinking the same thing." I brushed the crumbs off my face.

TREE-HUGGER

WHICH IS HOW I FOUND MYSELF at the top of an oak tree at dusk in Central Park. It was two o'clock by the time we finished the most awkward possible breakfast with the Fockers. At 5:30 John called Steven from the tree to check in. Helen told John that Steven was not in the office but that she had orders to transfer John to his cell phone immediately if he checked in.

"Where the hell have you been!?" I could hear how angry he was from across the tree.

"Farrah got hurt last night, and I had to get her inside quickly, and I lost cell service at our location."

"Where are you now?"

"We are walking, on our way to a more secure spot. I am going to try the equipment shed in Central Park after six p.m. when ops close for the day. We should be secure there for the night."

"Which shed?" Weird question, right?

"The one right off of Sheep Meadow."

"All right, be safe and call me in the morning."

Sitting in an oak tree at dusk in Central Park in April with the crush of your life is something I'd recommend to anyone. The air was crisp, there were pink and white blossoms on the trees, and we had found two perfect branches to accommodate us. I could see across Sheep Meadow and above it the Midtown skyline. I wondered if I could see the top of the building we'd stayed in. I wondered if I'd ever go back there. I wondered if John was for real or if this was a stress-induced romance. I decided I didn't care. Even though my life was for sure in danger and I was dealing with a side of humanity that I'd rather not know about, I felt happier than I had since I was a kid.

Two hours later it got dark and much less fun. I was freezing, my butt was numb, and my nerves were shot. Central Park is filled with a variety of animals during the night, human and otherwise, and they are all a little scary. But none were moving toward the shed with any intention of killing us and taking our precious diaper bag.

"This is ridiculous. Can't we just go back to your secret lair?"

"No, my parents are there. And we have to wait this out to see if the operation is secure."

I rolled my eyes. I'd had enough. "Right."

"You getting a little sick of this particular branch of the legal system, Digit?"

"Don't."

"You feeling a little up a tree?"

"Please."

"I'm going to go out on a limb here . . ."

Mercifully, the murderers arrived just then. Leaves rustled under the Japanese maple that was to the right of the shed. I couldn't make out how many there were, but I could see movement in the darkness. John grabbed my arm and motioned for me to be quiet. Duh, like I was the one making the corny jokes.

We sat, barely breathing for an excruciating ten minutes while whoever was there searched the shed and gave up. They walked back toward us, passing under our tree, and we could see that there were three of them, well covered in black clothes and baseball hats. There would be no way to identify them, except the first one stopped directly under our tree to make a phone call.

"Nothing to see here. They've disappeared." Shudder, shudder, punch.

ALCOHOL AND CALCULUS DON'T MIX.
NEVER DRINK AND DERIVE.

WE WAITED EXACTLY FIFTEEN MINUTES BEFORE we jumped out of our tree and raced back to safety on Seventy-ninth Street. We paused, listening for John's parents, when we got back into the warm foyer. We were relieved to see they were out, and John kissed me exactly six times before making a beeline for the intercom to the magic kitchen. I headed straight for my favorite spot in front of the fireplace, hoping someone would come light it for me. "I'm going to have another look in the diaper bag," I shouted into the next room. "It looks like nothing but pages of numbers, and the terrorists don't seem to want it. But if it was worth compromising Scarlet's whole suicide bombing and may have something to do with people wanting to kill us, it has to mean something to someone." I sat on the floor and spread the pages out in front of me. John called down to William for tea. Now, I feel like I'm old enough for an occasional beer, but tea? Am I really old enough to be sipping tea?

"You ready to fill me in?"

I jumped at the voice. John's dad had walked in off of the terrace and stood behind the wing chair across from me. He was a very scary man, a fact that was amplified by his King Kong frame and his laser eyes. I imagined being interrogated by him and confessing to excessive body hair and impure thoughts about his son.

He saw that he'd terrified me and softened. "Listen, Farrah, I have a feeling you guys are in worse trouble than you bargained for. If you're hiding from the good guys *and* the bad guys, you're in over your head."

John walked in with an actual silver tea tray and froze when he saw his dad. "Hi, Dad. I, uh, we didn't know you were here. Where's Mom?"

"Your mom got called out on a job. She'll be out about three weeks, classified location."

"Of course." There was an awkward silence while John looked for someplace to put the tea and tried not to meet his dad's eyes.

"Johnny, I think you need my help. You can't hide here forever, and you have a lot of people looking for you, your girlfriend, and whatever's in that bag."

"She's not my girlfriend." Ouch. "She's underage."

"Until June." Jeez! I wait this long to say a word, and this is what I come out with? Does anyone have a muzzle in this mansion? I might as well have said, "Mr. Bennett, right now I am seventeen, but in a few weeks I am going to legally jump your son." No more talking for me; I went back to the papers.

Mr. Bennett was smirking like he was reading my mind. Maybe he could—doesn't the CIA employ people who can do stuff like that? I didn't stand a chance.

"June twenty-second, isn't it?"

I didn't say anything. He must have run a check on me while we were up our tree. It made sense. I was a stranger in his house who was compromising his son's career.

"There are a few benefits to being in the CIA." He let me sit with that for a bit and turned his attention to John. "I know your operation is compromised. And you have, as you well know, an underage girl in your care and are responsible for her well-being. Her parents could sue the Bureau or you. It's not like you to deviate from operating procedure, and, as this is your first real field assignment, I'm more than a little curious as to the details of this operation and why you've picked now to go AWOL."

"Dad, I have it under control."

"You have a group of terrorists trying to kill your girl-fri—sorry, your assignment—and you seem to be hiding from the FBI. Is that what passes for under control in your book?" Mr. Bennett was trying unsuccessfully not to raise his voice.

"No." John sat down and put his head in his hands. He looked like it physically hurt him to ask for help. "Okay, Dad. This is what we know: There was a terror organization communicating through a Los Angeles television station. Farrah's involvement began when she cracked their communication system. She can make a positive identification of one of their operatives, who is a known member of the Jonas Furnis organization. The FBI staged a fake kidnapping to get her into protective custody. This group was responsible for the recent events at JFK, and Farrah and I believe that two of their operatives working out of New York were at the heart of the operation. They'd been under suspicion, and their calls had been remotely monitored by the FBI for some time. We believe that the woman was the suicide bomber and that she left the diaper bag for her partner so he could continue to blackmail the person they call Britney, who's been helping them but is also double-crossing Jonas Furnis in some way. That's where we get a little murky."

"What are those papers? They just look like numbers, no text?"

I realized he was talking to me. "Oh, yeah, they are just streams of numbers. The left column is a stream of nine-digit numbers. The right column has numbers of various lengths ranging from four to seven digits. At first I thought that these numbers were an encoding of names or locations, but now I see that the left column is a list of eight-digit numbers with a check digit at the end . . ."

Mr. Bennett shot John a *Huh?* with his eyes. John smiled a

little. "She's not normal, Dad." He got up and started stacking wood in the fireplace.

Like it's the first time I've ever heard that. I ignored him. "So the left column is probably a list of nine-digit bank routing numbers. Yes, you can see here that some of them appear more than once. The right column is probably the amount deposited to each bank. This could be some sort of accounting of how they are financing their operations."

"So, that sounds incredibly valuable to the FBI—why don't you just hand all this over to Steven and go home?"

John and I were quiet for a second. I finally spit it out. "Because Steven's trying to kill us."

John was squirming in his big leather chair. Not only was the chair oversize, but John seemed to be shrinking under his dad's amused gaze. "I'm sorry, son. I'm trying to follow you, but now you're telling me that the real villain is your boss? I've known Steven a long time . . ."

"I know. We don't understand it either. But every time we tell him our whereabouts, a bunch of goons comes after us. It's almost like he sent us to New York to get us out from under the FBI's protection and into harm's way. And the last time we checked in, we gave him a phony location and guess who showed up leading the goons?"

"Steven?" John's dad was horrified and sat quietly for a while. "I remember how concerned everyone was when he was taken prisoner by those eco-nuts. He came home a hero when he was finally released, but he was never the same."

John answered, "And isn't it kind of weird that he *was* released? Why would they torture him and then send him home? I keep wondering if there was some reason that they wanted him safe and sound, back running the hunt for terrorists inside the FBI."

"You're saying Steven is a spy for Jonas Furnis." It wasn't a question, just a statement as Mr. Bennett ran through all the facts. "You're going to have to come up with some pretty solid proof before you find yourself fired, arrested, or dead."

"I've got none." John looked exhausted.

"I might." They seemed to have forgotten all about me, sitting by the fire, buried in paper. "Well, sort of. I don't know how we prove that Steven is working for Jonas Furnis. Steven's trying to kill us and Jonas Furnis is trying to kill us, so it's safe to assume that he is working for them. He's been trying to kill us ever since we got this diaper bag, and the only living people who know about this diaper bag are Luke and Britney." Light bulb. I looked over at John and saw that he'd had the same thought. "Steven's Britney. And I think he's stealing from them."

"Okay. Go on." John's dad was incapable of treating me like a fruitcake. I was starting to love this man.

"These papers are definitely a financial record. They are lists of bank routing numbers, as I said before, accounting for money going into international banks. On their own, I can see why the bad guys would want them back because they probably show how they're paying for all their bombings and stuff."

"Okay, so if Steven's working for Jonas Furnis, I can see why he'd want those back. But why do you think he's stealing from them?"

"Like I said before, bank routing numbers have nine digits, with the last number being a check digit at the end. The error-checking system requires that the sum of the check sequence has to be zero on a mod-10 clock. That's how you know if it's a real bank ID or not."

"Lost you." John was giving me the fruitcake look again, but his dad was expressionless.

"I might need paper."

John got up to get paper and a pencil from a writing desk in the corner. Before he handed it to me, he turned to his dad and smiled. "You're not going to believe this."

We all gathered around the coffee table, and I started writing the numbers out as I was talking, going through each formula. I knew they were not going to take my word for it. "A mod-10 clock is like a regular clock, numbered 1 through 12, except that it's numbered 1 through 10 — 10 and all of its multiples being equivalent to zero. Just like you never get to 13 on a regular clock, you start over at 1 instead, making 12 just like zero." They were nodding. I went on. "If you label each of the nine digits as n1, n2, n3, n4, n5, n6, n7, n8, n9, and then you multiply each number by 7, 3, and 9, repeating three times, you get the formula:

$$7n1 + 3n2 + 9n3 + 7n4 + 3n5 + 9n6 + 7n7 + 3n8 + 9n9$$

When you work that out, the sum should be equivalent to zero mod-10. Or more simply, just divisible by 10. So look at this one. The bank routing number is 114706225. It's a fake routing number."

Mr. Bennett looked at John for a reality check. "I saw the SAT scores but . . ."

"She's amazing, right?" John smiled at me, and I completely forgot what we were talking about.

"Go on." Mr. Bennett was on the edge of his seat, like he was waiting for the punch line.

"You looked up my SAT scores?" I felt completely naked.

"Farrah, I'm sorry, but I had to know whom I was dealing with. It's part of my job. And they're certainly nothing to be ashamed of. Now keep going."

I let it go. "Well, some of the check digits don't check. This one in particular shows up six times. If you use the formula you get:

$$(7{*}1) + (3{*}1) + (9{*}4) + (7{*}7) + (3{*}0) + (9{*}6) + (7{*}2) + (3{*}2) + (9{*}5)$$

The sum is 214, not divisible by 10. The check digit should be 9, making the sum 250."

"Let me try." To my surprise, Mr. Bennett took the pencil

from me and worked through the formula both ways, with 5 as the check digit and then with 9. Satisfied, he put the pencil down. "Okay, I see. And you're telling me that you did all that in your head?"

"Yes."

Amazing. He called me amazing. In front of his dad. Who knows my SAT scores. I had never been so fully out of the closet. Was I going to be his girlfriend and get invited on family vacations?

"Farrah, you're saying that you have an accounting of terror financing with some deposits going into fake banks? How much money is missing?"

Oh, I checked back in. I took a few minutes to identify all the phony money orders and added them up. "Almost six million dollars. Someone's going to be pissed."

John stood up and started pacing, head down and hands behind his back. He really needed a pipe to make the whole thing work. He was thinking out loud. "And that's why Steven's been trying to kill us ever since we got the bag? It's the only explanation that makes sense. Steven had sent Scarlet an accounting ledger, never thinking that she'd pick up on the fact that there was money missing. Didn't she say she got it in an e-mail or something?"

I nodded. "I think so. It was supposed to prove to her that there was support for what they were doing. Which makes sense — he'd want her to see how much money they were putting into their operation if she was doubting how important the bombing was to the cause. And Steven would have never thought she'd pick up on the missing money, but then she started blackmailing him."

We went through our options over and over again, weighing the risks (getting killed) and benefits (cleaning out the FBI and ending world terror). John and his dad settled into a relaxed dialogue, where they were both adults and professionals. It reminded me of how it was with my dad and the respect he showed me when I was working something out.

I felt simultaneously a little homesick and a little grown-up. And besides the fact that I was being hunted by friend and foe alike, I liked the feeling of operating in this world where I could jump in and think as hard as I wanted.

John was running scenarios. "If we get a copy of these documents to the terrorists, they'll have Steven killed immediately. If we get them to the CIA, they'll spend the next five years conducting an investigation into bank accounts that will be closed in a matter of hours."

Mr. Bennett agreed. "Going after the terrorists with this information is a waste of time. If we're lucky, we'll get three guys arrested. But I'm sure Steven has all the information the CIA needs to break this terror cell up on a large scale. He'd keep records for his own protection. His full cooperation will take years off of any investigation."

John was pacing again. "But how do we have him arrested? These routing numbers on their own are not exactly a smoking gun. They prove that money is missing, but they won't prove that Steven was the one stealing it."

"Can't you call the FBI with this and have someone rifle through his desk or search his computer or something?" I admit, everything I know about crime fighting I learned on TV.

John looked at me patiently. "We could, but there's no one to call. We don't know who else is involved there, and if we show our hand to the wrong guy, Steven disappears and we've got nothing. We can't even try to trap him in the FBI building because anyone in security could be working with him and turn on us."

"So, we are nowhere?" My spirits were starting to sink. "The diaper bag alone proves nothing; we can't find more proof without risking getting caught . . . We might as well just hand the bag over to the terrorists and let them have at Steven. At least we'd have removed their spy at the FBI."

Mr. Bennett smiled at me. "You're right—the diaper bag only has power to take Steven down in the hands of the terrorists. That's what we have to threaten him with."

John sat down next to me in front of the fire. "Right. He has to know we have the ledger, and he has to need our protection. But we have to confront him alone, without any other FBI agents who could be in on it, where he will feel like it's safe to turn over his evidence."

"Should we invite him over?" I sounded like my mom.

"Not exactly. But we need to arrange a meeting where he will feel comfortable coming alone." John refilled my tea like we were recounting the highs and lows of the afternoon's fox hunt.

"If you guys call, he'll just bring his friends to kill you. Johnny, I've seen you shoot, so let's avoid a shootout at all costs. We need someone else to initiate a private meeting." Mr. Bennett looked my way. "How about your mom? I see she's an accomplished actress."

THERE'S NO EMOTICON FOR
WHAT I'M FEELING

᪥

MR. BENNETT ANNOUNCED THAT WE'D LEAVE for Los Angeles in two hours. I assumed he meant we'd leave the townhouse in two hours, until John came downstairs with our bags and called the secret elevator. Two hours? How is that possible? How did you book a flight, get to the airport, clear security, choose a day-old sandwich, board the plane, and take off in two hours? It didn't make any sense, and I watched the clock as we sped via Lincoln Town Car to JFK. It turns out there's a whole different world out there, previously hidden from me, called flying private. Mr. Bennett called his pilot from the car, and we pulled up to his plane in forty-five minutes. We were fully fueled with our flight plan approved, and twenty minutes later we were eating crab salad at twenty thousand feet. I could get used to this.

Of course, the irony wasn't lost on me. What would Jonas Furnis think about our mode of travel? Three passengers on a plane that could easily carry fifty. I didn't know how many gallons of fuel we were each burning, but I'm sure it would make me sick. But we were in a hurry, and the plane was waiting for us. And we were on a mission that could certainly justify it, right? Maybe. But I'm sure everyone can come up with a reason they're driving a huge gas-guzzler (I have a lot of stuff to schlep), wearing shoes made out of an endangered rhino (they match my bag), or not recycling the peanut butter jar (it's a pain). I was as guilty as anyone.

The flight attendant was cheery and efficient. I couldn't take my eyes off her as she brought us warm nuts and drinks. I pictured Scarlet, dressed much the same way, pouring a little champagne and knowing exactly what she was about to do. Did she feel compassion for those children, or did their little faces fuel her rage? How angry would a person have to be to do something like this? I didn't relax until the flight attendant took her seat near the cockpit.

John and I sat together in the back row, and his dad was seated at the front of the plane but in a rear-facing seat with a table. He had three newspapers spread out in front of him. He was immersed in the *Financial Times,* but I could tell he was being careful not to look at us. I don't know if it was the fact that Mr. Bennett seemed to have approved of me or that it was just so obvious that something was up between us, but John majorly let down his guard. He covered us both in a blanket and held my hand under it in the most normal possible way, like we'd been married for thirty years.

And I wasn't really that worried about what Mr. Bennett thought, anyway. I was starting to care less and less about what anybody thought. Honestly, I had stopped caring about so many of the things that had been critical to my existence a week ago. Working to fit in had been the central focus of my life, and now I fit with John with no effort at all. And maybe with his dad too. It made me feel like there might be a whole world of people out there, waiting to accept me or even like me. If we could just get through the next twenty-four hours.

Mr. Bennett had called my mom from his scrambled and undetectable CIA phone. He was very careful with what he shared—nothing about the diaper bag or the ledgers, just that it was critical that we got Steven to agree to come to a meeting alone and suspecting nothing. His idea was that she would call his office and tell him that she'd had enough of her daughter being taken across the country hunting terrorists, that she was hysterical with worry, and that she wanted to go to the press and tell them that it was all a sham. He wouldn't care if she did because he and the terrorists knew it was a fake, anyway, but to keep up Bureau appearances, he would humor her by coming by for a cup of coffee.

She made the call immediately, and we waited during most of the flight to hear back from her. "Jeez, Digit, can your mom talk or what? Why is this taking so long?" John was elbowing me in my seat.

"You have no idea. My guess is that she got into the role of hysterical mom and just ran with it. She'll call us before we land, but she'll need time to regroup first. Method acting."

She called Mr. Bennett about three hours into our flight. "Oh, Henry, it was perfect. He bought the whole thing and thinks I just need a good talking to and a stiff drink. Who could blame me? He'll be here tomorrow morning to calm my fears. Shall I stay in character?"

"Thank you, Rebecca. We'll be at your house tonight. No, there's no reason to be too secretive about it—the terrorists all think we are in New York. It's just your neighbors we have to hide from to keep the kidnapping story alive. Yes, she's fine. She's quite a compelling girl." He looked over in time to catch John brushing a piece of my hair out of my eyes. "John and I are both quite taken with her. Okay, see you tonight. Call me on this number if you need anything."

At one point during the flight, John got up to go to the bathroom and his dad came back to sit in his place. "May I?" he asked.

Uh, it's your plane. "Sure," I said.

He seemed to start in the middle of a conversation, one I hadn't been in on until now. "It's really nice to be with family. John's made the best of this life, moving around all the time and starting over. He seems to have adapted to it pretty well. I always wonder if he'll end up choosing a more predictable life."

I had absolutely no light to shed on John in this respect. "Did you ever think you'd have a different kind of job?"

"Not really. I was with the FBI before the CIA, which is the same sort of job. I was chosen for a very prestigious area of the FBI at one point—Special Sector—a very high-profile position."

Just then John came back and took the seat next to his dad. "Dad, you're not really telling this story again . . ."

"It's my story, John. And I love telling it." Mr. Bennett turned his body toward me, as if John's mockery just lost him the right to hear. "When I was offered the position, I had just begun a relationship with Mrs. Bennett. We were wildly in love, and I knew almost immediately that I wanted to spend my life with her. She was living in New York at the time, and I was commuting on the weekends from Washington, D.C. The job in Special Sector meant working seven days a week, and there would be no room for a relationship."

"So what did you do?" Newly in love myself, I was riveted.

"It wasn't easy. I had been offered their highest honor, and to refuse it would be career suicide. I knew that if I didn't take the job, there would be no place left for me at the FBI."

"Ever?"

"Never. But I just told them the truth. I said this . . ."

"Here we go." John was rolling his eyes.

"I said this: I've fallen in love, and if I don't find out where this is going, I know I will regret it for the rest of my life."

I looked over to see John mouthing the last few words like a twelve-year-old.

"That's the most romantic thing I've ever heard." I meant it.

Mr. Bennett smiled. "You know, Farrah, I've told him that story a thousand times, but I don't know if he's ever heard me."

"What do you mean?" John was a little hurt.

"It was a small price to pay for a lifetime with your mother. At some point, you have to make decisions with your heart, get off your plan. Johnny here has had his heart pretty well locked away."

"Yeah, Dad, I'm a robot. Anything else Farrah needs to know about me? Any baby pictures you want to show her before we get back to work?"

"Nah," Mr. Bennett said, lifting himself out of the seat between us. "She's got it all pretty well figured out."

Did I?

THERE'S NO PLACE LIKE HOME

WE LANDED AT LAX AND HOPPED into a much more subtle ride. It was a Toyota sedan or maybe a Honda. It was the sort of navy blue car that you would never notice driving down your street. It was so strange being back in L.A. I'd only been gone for a few days, but the warm air, palm trees, and strip malls on the ride from the airport welcomed me home. Mr. Bennett sat in the front seat with the driver, so there was no reason why John couldn't hold me in the back seat all the way to Santa Monica.

"You tired?" he whispered.

"Probably." *More like love-stoned,* I thought.

"It'll be good for you to be home tonight. Sleep in your own bed."

"I'd rather sleep in your own bed."

"I hadn't thought about that." He laughed and silently kissed the side of my neck. "How are we going to fill your parents in on FBI protocol? I haven't slept more than two feet from my charge during this whole operation."

Mr. Bennett turned around and said over his shoulder, "Don't kid yourselves. They'll figure you two out in about one minute. You don't have to be a trained spy to see what's brewing back there. I'm sure the Higginses have a suitable sofa for you, John."

So much for whispering. John and I sat silently like a couple of scolded kids. Mr. Bennett turned back around, hiding his smile.

We got off the 405 at the Wilshire Boulevard exit and took the Wilshire West ramp to get to Santa Monica. I flashed back to the last time I'd been exactly here, driving over the speed limit away from that creepy Jonas Furnis guy. I'd made a split-second decision — the kind that was supposed to be your best, the voice of your true inner guidance — and made a horrible mistake to take the ramp that led west, away from the police department. I wondered where I would be if I'd taken the right ramp on that very first day of this ordeal. I would have ended up at the Beverly Hills Police Department, just as I'd meant to. I would never have seen John again but would have met a guy named Officer Dudley, not cute in a cheap suit, who would have taken my statement and sent me home to certain death. I squeezed John's hand, grateful for bad decisions, wrong turns, and my quirky inner guidance.

We made our way into Santa Monica and onto my quiet street. I was struck by how beautiful it was. The street was lined with ficus trees that had been there for a hundred years. The houses were a mix; some Spanish architecture, some Cape Cod, some Colonials, some brand-new and ginormous. I smiled when we reached my traditional Colonial-style house, painted French blue with an absolutely asymmetric fig tree in the front yard. It wasn't Park Avenue, but it was home.

It was nearly ten o'clock and the street was deserted. No cameras, no bad guys. The driver pulled into the driveway, and I led John and his dad to the back door. I hesitated with my hand on the knob. What was John going to think of my parents, my eclectic-at-best house, and my bedroom? Oh God, what was he going to think of my bedroom? And he thought I wasn't normal before.

My dad was waiting for us, unlocked the door, and ushered us in. All the shades and shutters were closed. I fell without thinking into his arms and held him for a long time. I like that my dad, like me, has a uniform: khaki pants, light blue button-down shirt, brown belt, and shoes. Simple and perfect.

"Dad, this is Henry Bennett and John Bennett, and this is my dad, Ben Higgins. Where's Mom?"

Always on cue, she made her entrance. Nice choices for a fake kidnapping reunion meeting—I don't know how she does it. She was in gray pencil skirt that just brushed her knees, with a pale pink cashmere sweater tucked in and cinched by a thin alligator belt. Her slightly heeled loafers were a similar color leather, not matching—no, never matching.

"Hellooo. You must be the Bennetts." She warmly shook one hand, then the other. "I'm Rebecca Higgins. Welcome to California."

She turned to me and hugged me, then took my hands in hers and took a step back to take me in. "You could do with a blow dry, but you look absolutely gorgeous. You even look rested somehow, if that's possible, and a little older."

Mr. Bennett answered for me, "She'll be eighteen in June." He gave me a wink. I'd never met someone who saw through me so completely.

Awkward is not in my mother's vocabulary. Before two beats passed, she led us down a few steps to the living room, where her 1920s-style low sofas flanked a large mirrored coffee table. She had set up a tray with an assortment of glasses, a bottle of red wine, and a tall elegant pitcher of lemonade. A small bowl of mixed nuts and a plate of shrimp cocktails completed the stage. And I mean stage—this is not how we live. But somehow Mom anticipated that these were shrimp-eating people we were dealing with. If only she knew.

We all started to take our seats. I sat down next to my dad and subconsciously placed my hand down to my other side, like I was saving the seat for John. He did not meet my eye but rather crossed the room to sit on the far side of the adjacent sofa next to my mom. So this was how it was going to be. Probably smart.

Because of the situation, the small talk lasted only a few

minutes. Lovely home, how long have you lived in Santa Monica, where is John's mother, et cetera. Out of nowhere we heard a crash from upstairs. John and Mr. Bennett were on their feet in a second, both reaching for their guns.

My dad was a little amused. "I'm sorry. I forgot to mention our son, Danny. He has recently taken up karate and has done more damage to the furniture in his room than you can imagine." He got up and shouted up the stairs, "Danny, Farrah's here. Come down and say hi."

John and his dad took a second to compose themselves, gave a little embarrassed laugh, and sat back down. Mr. Bennett said something to John in a language I didn't recognize, and they both laughed.

John explained to the rest of us. "There's an Iranian proverb: 'He who has been bitten by a snake fears a piece of string.'" Danny ran down the stairs, white karate sash tied around his forehead like Hong Kong Phooey. Absolutely ridiculous, but he couldn't have cared less.

"Digit!" He gave me a too-tight bear hug that really felt like he meant it. "Look at you, I thought you'd come back all vacant and kidnapped-looking. Are these the perps?"

John got up. "Hi, Danny. I'm John Bennett. This is my father, Henry Bennett."

"Cool. Hey." Danny shook their hands and plopped on the couch in the seat I'd hoped to save for John. I surveyed my previously innocent younger brother for signs that he'd been corrupted by *my* friend in *my* bikini. He looked more relaxed than ever, which was suspicious. "So what's the big plan?"

Mr. Bennett smiled at him and said, "Yes, let's get down to business. Rebecca, please, tell us what Steven said when you last spoke."

Deep breath, shoulders back, she was on. "Well, he initially resisted meeting here, said that it would be too likely that he would be spotted. I asked why it would seem strange that an FBI agent would be coming to the home of a kidnapped girl's parents. He had no argument."

"It's likely that he wanted a location that he could secure—home turf as it were." Mr. Bennett raised his glass of wine as he spoke, admiring the color, then sipping with approval. *Nice job, Mom.*

"That's what I thought. So I insisted that he come here, as my nerves are too raw to leave the house. He agreed to come here at nine a.m. tomorrow."

John tried to take control of the mission back from his dad. "Our plan is very simple. Steven will not be expecting me to be here, so I can use the element of surprise to disarm him. We will present him with the diaper bag and offer that he can either cooperate with us and give up Jonas Furnis, or we will turn the documents over to them ourselves. Assuming a normal survival instinct, he will cooperate, and we will arrange to move him into questioning and then witness protection."

My dad said, "That all makes sense. Where will Farrah be during this meeting? I don't want any harm to come her way in case there is a scuffle."

"Her safety is my utmost concern as well . . ." John started.

"You have no idea," Mr. Bennett said under his breath.

John ignored him. "We will have her secluded in an interior room, preferably upstairs."

"Well, then," my mom began, "I'm sure you are all exhausted. Henry, let me show you to the guest room. And, Farrah, you can show John to your room."

Awkward silence. Awkward silence. My dad jumped in to answer the question. "Farrah, you can bunk in with Danny tonight."

"Of course." I was relieved and disappointed. Everything about this was so weird. "Come on, John, it's this way." He followed me upstairs and into the small hallway that contained my room and my parents'. We stood outside my door for a second, my hand on the doorknob. He was smiling, and I was panicked. Was this the final step? Did anyone really need to know me *that* well? Couldn't some of my idiosyncrasies be kept in the dark?

John was laughing. He put his hand on mine and turned the knob. "This I've got to see."

He pushed the door open and there it was, in all its glory. Four walls and part of a ceiling covered in automobile poetry. It still struck me as beautiful as I took it in through John's eyes. I appreciated the even way I'd affixed them all to the wall, the reasonably even distribution of colors around the room. But still, it was a little over the top.

John walked around silently, running his fingers over every bumper sticker as he read them. After a few minutes, he turned to me and proclaimed, "You are one crazy chick." He pulled me into his arms and kissed me. I kicked the door shut behind me and kissed him back like it might be the last time. My instincts were right again.

IT'S AS BAD AS YOU THINK, AND THEY ARE OUT TO GET YOU

AFTER AS MUCH POSSIBLE TIME BEHIND closed doors, I went out into the hall and said too loudly, "Okay, John, looks like you have everything you need in there. So I guess that's it." John grabbed my hand, trying to make me stay. "Don't go through my stuff," I whispered.

"Me? Never." He said it like he'd already decided which drawer he'd start with. He shut the door.

I found myself still wide awake at two a.m., checking the clock over Danny's trophy wall for any signs of morning. How could I be expected to sleep? First of all, John was all the way across the hall—too far away to smell and likely reading my trigonometry journal (don't ask!). Plus there was tomorrow morning's showdown with the terrorist sympathizer who was trying to have me killed. Remember that?

I fell asleep around 3:30, so by the time I woke up, everyone besides Danny was already dressed and downstairs. I snuck across the hall to my room, hoping to find John but instead finding a neatly made bed. I took a shower in my very own bathroom and got dressed in front of my very own closet. I was stumped by so many clothing choices, so I went with a pair of jeans identical to the ones I'd been wearing all week and a brown version of the same T-shirt. Clean socks, boots on, ready to go. I found everyone sitting around the breakfast table, eating pancakes and bacon, sipping coffee, and getting acquainted. I got myself some orange juice and sat down next to John.

"Nice way to mix it up," he said, noticing my clean but nearly identical clothes.

"Ha-ha." I filled my plate with bacon and dug in.

My dad was asking Mr. Bennett a thousand questions. "So if you live in New York and Connecticut, where do you file your tax return?" Uh, who cares?

"We file in New York, as we are seldom in Connecticut and mostly out of the country."

"Do you go through a special line when you go through customs?" Was this really necessary?

Mr. Bennett was all patience. "We do if we are reentering the country while not on assignment. But if we are on assignment, we have to go through the normal line so that we appear to be civilians."

"So you have fake passports?" Oh, good. Now my mom was grilling him too.

"Yes, we have several sets of falsified documents that help us to move freely and undetected around the world. Now, Rebecca, tell me about your acting. Are you working now?" And with that, my mom took the stage. I watched her speak, without listening to what she was saying. I marveled at how comfortable she was in her skin, like a palm tree whose roots are so deep that it can sway and bend in impossible ways but always comes back to its center, tall and graceful. I wondered if this is what made her a good actress, this total knowledge and comfort with who she was. It was as if she could go as far as she wanted because she had this sense of herself to draw her back.

John was watching me watching her. He caught my eye and gave me a little wink that made my heart race. I was sure I was blushing and was so grateful that my mom had my dad and Mr. Bennett so completely captivated.

At 8:00 Danny rolled in and finished all the food on everyone's plate. "So when does the bad guy get here?" He was as casual as ever, but the question seemed to put everyone a bit on edge. After John and I finished the breakfast dishes and the parents passed sections of three newspapers around, there was nothing to do but wait for our prey. Winking John was long gone; future FBI chief John was here to stay. He sat still in the living room, checking to make sure his gun was still in its holster exactly every 3.5 minutes. I was grateful to him for the regularity of this habit, feeling lulled by the rhythm. The anxiety in the room was such that any 3, 3.5, 3, 2, 3.5 pattern would have sent me over the edge.

Mr. Bennett decided that the safest place for me to hide was our only windowless room, the downstairs bathroom. It put me closer than they'd like to where they would be confronting Steven, but it was the best defense in case he did not actually come alone and they tried to shoot through windows. At 8:55 Danny and I were placed in the bathroom, John and Mr. Bennett were concealed on either side of the TV armoire in the living room, and my parents were seated on the couch, as if waiting for dinner guests.

At 9:10 there was a knock on the kitchen door. Showtime. I heard my mom cross the living room into the kitchen and open the door. "Hello, Steven. Thank you so much for coming, I have really been a wreck. Come in and sit down . . ." Whack, stumble, male scream, a minute passes.

"Guys, you can come out now." At Dad's instruction, Danny and I went into the living room to see what was going on.

Steven was seated in a kitchen chair, each hand cuffed behind him to a wooden spindle. He was completely disoriented and seemed to be scanning the room for the person who would make sense of this.

"Care to explain this to me?" He was talking to John. "How did you get back to California, and why am I cuffed?" He did the shudder, shudder, but the punch just strained his bound hands.

John was pacing in front of him. "We have the diaper bag;

we know what's in it. We know that you sent us to New York to die and that you even came to the shed in Central Park to kill us yourself. We know you have been stealing from Jonas Furnis and were blackmailed. And we know that you'll be dead or worse as soon as we pass the diaper bag on to them. That's what's going on."

Steven went white. Literally, all the color drained from his face, and he looked very ill. He hung his head, maybe deciding what to say, for a few minutes. When he looked up, he addressed John. "I really did want to protect her, to keep her from enduring what I did in captivity. I wanted her in hiding for protection. I thought you'd have a little fun thinking you were fighting crime. I never read the transcripts. I didn't even know Scarlet had been taped. Everyone knew that Jonas Furnis was running out of money, and she was getting cold feet thinking that she'd sacrificed her life for a cause that was going to go broke anyway. I was told to send her the ledger to show her how much had been spent on the bombing already and how much was still there. I had no idea she'd be able to figure out that I was stealing — she was just an angry young mother."

"Mother of who?" As much as I wanted to fade away into the wall I was leaning against, I needed to know.

Steven looked my way. "She wasn't much older than you, but she had a child. He was born with a severe birth defect believed to be caused by toxins in our environment. She left the baby with her mother to join up with Jonas Furnis. They knew they could use her anger for their mission."

John was calm. "The blackmail money was for the baby." Steven nodded. "But why even involve us? When we told you we knew where the bag was, you could have just gone to get it yourself."

Steven smiled sadly. "You already knew too much about Scarlet. And I couldn't run the risk that there was enough information in there to help you find Luke. What was I going to do if you got Luke arrested? He'd identify me the second he was in custody. Plus I knew that if Farrah had ten minutes with that ledger, she would see through it. I had to get you out from under FBI protection so you could . . . die. I alerted Jonas Furnis that you were on to Scarlet and Luke, but when they failed to kill you, I had no other alternative but to come kill you myself."

Mr. Bennett shook his head. "Steven, we started our careers together. How did you ever get so far off track that you're helping terrorists?"

"What would you do, Henry? I knew that if I ever defied them, they'd go after my parents, my children, everyone. And I figured I could work for both sides for a while. They're really running out of money. And if I could take a little for myself, I'd speed up their collapse and make it worth my while, too . . . I don't know. I thought it was a way out."

Mr. Bennett pulled a chair around and sat down so that he and Steven were knee to knee. "I feel sorry for you, Steven, I really do. God knows what you went through in captivity; God knows how broken you are inside. No one could expect your moral compass to be perfectly tuned after all that. I have always believed you were a good man. But now you have aided Jonas Furnis in a horrible bombing, and you have tried to kill my son and an innocent girl. It's time to make things right." Man, he was good.

Steven hung his head again and started to cry. It was a silent cry, complete with real tears and small sobs. It seemed like it had been a long time coming. The master of patience and control, Mr. Bennett waited until he stopped and looked up. "Are you ready to help us?"

"What do you want from me?" Steven asked.

"First, I want you to call your contact at Jonas Furnis and tell them that Farrah is dead. Tell them that you found her in New York and you killed her yourself. Two shots to the head and the body in the East River. They are not to worry about her identifying them ever again."

I shuddered. My dad motioned for me to come sit between my mom and him on the couch. I was grateful. Danny sat across from us, wide-eyed and maybe understanding how much danger I was in for the first time.

"Fine. You have my phone. Under contacts, hit Dry Cleaner." John picked up his phone and started scrolling down the contact list. He pressed Dry Cleaner and the speaker, then held the phone in front of Steven.

"Yeah?" was the answer.

"It's me. I've got her. Well, I mean I had her, took care of her, and dumped her in the river . . ."

"Which river?"

"East River. She's gone. We can get back to work." Steven looked around at us for approval. I kind of did feel sorry for the guy.

"Good, because there's a major hit today at two. Casualties in the hundreds, high profile. This is a breakthrough for us, so I'll call you in thirty minutes with the details. It's already set in motion, but we'll need you on the back end for cleanup in case there's evidence."

"Fine, we'll talk then." Steven nodded at John to hang up. He was whiter than before.

I felt my body go cold. "There's another attack tonight? Will we be able to stop this one? If we know about it in a half-hour, we'll have time, right? Right?"

Mr. Bennett was as smooth as silk. "Of course, Farrah, Steven will help us. He is also going to help us gather all the documentation that we need to find, arrest, and convict every member of the Jonas Furnis organization. Steven, I assume you have been keeping some sort of records, just in case."

"In case," Steven repeated. "I'm tired. I've been hiding forever. John, I have heart medication in my front shirt pocket. Would you please give it to me, and then I will tell you what you need to know."

John looked at his dad, who nodded. He reached into Steven's pocket and pulled out a prescription vial and handed it to his dad. Mr. Bennett read aloud, "Nitrostat. It's nitro-glycerin. Steven, are you having chest pains?" Steven nodded and stuck out his tongue, waiting for it. It was eerie, a grown man cuffed with his hands behind him, seated calmly with his tongue out, incapable of even punching one fingerless fist into the other. John placed the pill on his tongue and Steven swallowed it and smiled. "That's better."

"John, if you go into my office, there is a set of seven filing cabinets behind my desk. The last one is labeled 'Personal' with a padlock on it. The code is 1-2-3-4."

"Your secret code is 1-2-3-4?" I was appalled.

"I have wanted to get caught for a long time." He coughed a few times before going on. "You'll find a file called 'Utility Bills.' It's everything you need to take Jonas Furnis down for good."

He dropped his head again, but this time he seemed to be concealing pain. "I'm sorry, John. I betrayed you, and you are a good agent."

"Thanks, Steven. I'm sorry about everything you've been through." John put his hand on Steven's shoulder. Could this get any heavier? Apparently so. John said, "Steven? Steven? Dad? I think he's dead."

Mr. Bennett got up slowly, almost like he didn't want to get where he was going. He lifted Steven's head and gently touched his neck and nodded.

Danny gasped. "Dude. He's dead?"

"That pill he took must have been some form of arsenic or succinylcholine or something. Marked to look like Nitrostat. I wonder how long he's been carrying it around in his pocket, fighting the urge to take it." Mr. Bennett started to uncuff him.

My dad said, "Poor guy, it must be a lot of work to live a lie."

Mr. Bennett, John, and I all responded at the same time; "It is."

THE WORLD IS COMING TO AN END. PLEASE LOG OFF.

⌒

WITH STEVEN'S DEAD BODY LYING IN the middle of my living room, we all sat around and contemplated what to do. Dad immediately suggested we call the police or the FBI to get his body out of the house. I couldn't have agreed more, but Mr. Bennett reminded us of the bigger issue.

"There's another terror attack planned for today at two p.m. We have seven minutes until we receive a call that will reveal all of the details. No one must know that Steven is dead." Mr. Bennett and John were fully in charge now, barely keeping my parents and me in the loop. They were pacing next to one another, nodding and talking. Danny and I were more than a little freaked out by the dead body and gave up listening early on.

We all jumped when we heard a knock on the kitchen door, followed by the sound of the knob turning and footsteps across the linoleum floor. John drew his gun but stopped when he saw Olive bouncing into the living room, clad in running shorts, a tank top, and *my* bikini. "What? Danny? Aren't we going—" First she saw me, then she saw the dead body. "Farrah! Oh my God! I knew you were okay. Who's . . . ? What's going on here?" She stood there with her hands on her hips, as if the explanation that we owed her were the most urgent thing we had to deal with.

I tried to explain. "Yeah, we've had a bit of a situation here and I've had to hide, but it seems like it's going to be okay now. Well, not for him. He's dead. But he's expecting a call . . ."

Danny stopped my rambling by leading her over to the couch and sitting her down. "She caught some bad guys; he's one. She's safe now, but the really bad guys are about to do something worse." I marveled at his simplicity. That would have taken me twenty minutes to explain. But if I'd been doing the explaining, I wouldn't have been holding her hand. What's been going on around here?

Steven's phone rang just as I was about to ask. Mr. Bennett flipped it to speaker and answered with an indistinct "Yeah?"

"Okay. You got a pen?"

"Yeah," he mumbled.

John actually did have a pen and scribbled as the voice on the phone read from a list of letters: MODMIYKIFDBTAPZM-DIBIVHY.

"Got it?" the voice asked.

Mr. Bennett looked at me for confirmation. I nodded. "Yeah," he said, and hung up.

"Great. Another code. Like we have time for this. We have four hours until a major incident, and the guy can't just spit it out." John was finally losing it.

Mr. Bennett kept his cool. "Steven must have known how to crack this code. Farrah? Ben? Does this mean anything to you?"

Dad shook his head. "Not right off the bat. Farrah, let's get to it." We got up and walked instinctively to the game table, the same table that we sat at doing puzzles when I was two, solving differential equations at five. It was our table, a sacred space of thought. John handed us the sheet of paper and backed away, respectfully. Four hours and counting.

MODMIYKIFDBTAPZMDIBIVHY. We each sounded it out on our own. Mod Mike if the Beta Pez Midy Bivhy? We sounded it out backwards. We converted it into a numeric value using the alphabet, where A is worth one, and Z is worth twenty-six. Nothing.

Three hours and counting. The letters spun in circles in front of me, and the order was not coming. I didn't know if it was the exhaustion, the stress, or what, but the part of my mind that normally takes over was not kicking into gear. I arranged the letters vertically, took out the repeating letters. Nothing.

Two hours and counting. I was starting to panic. It was like my computer was frozen, but this wasn't a game. I'd be like the game show contestant who spits out the answer just after the buzzer goes off. But instead of a lovely parting gift, I'd have "casualties in the hundreds" on my conscience. I'd never sleep again.

John was pacing, playing the role of coach. "What do we know about these guys?" he asked. "You cracked their last code practically in your sleep, right? Maybe you're overthinking this. Could it just be another Fiorucci?"

"Fibonacci," my dad corrected him. And he slowly lifted his gaze to meet mine. "Ever since *The Da Vinci Code*," he said, smiling, "everyone's a . . ."

" . . . genius." we said together. It was an old joke between us. My dad and I had been working through ancient puzzles and mysteries forever, but as soon as *The Da Vinci Code* was published, everyone in the world thought that they were a cryptologist. Jonas Furnis was a fan of Fibonacci for sure.

"I checked that. There's no Fibonacci sequence in the numbers that corresponded to the letters, no matter how I arrange them." But I figured I'd give Fibonacci another try. I started to plow through it, step by step. "Okay, try this. We take the basic Fibonacci sequence, under 26, 1, 1, 2, 3, 5, 8, 13, 21, and convert it into letters using the 26-character alphabet: AABCEHMU. Right?"

My dad nodded and went on. "AABCEHMU. It could be a

series of Caesar shifts. Write it vertically." So I took the paper and wrote:

A
A
B
C
E
H
M
U

And then filled in the alphabet using a series of Caesar shifts, which begin the alphabet at the letter that begins each row on the left:

ABCDEFGHIJKLMNOPQRSTUVWXYZ
ABCDEFGHIJKLMNOPQRSTUVWXYZ
BCDEFGHIJKLMNOPQRSTUVWXYZA
CDEFGHIJKLMNOPQRSTUVWXYZAB
EFGHIJKLMNOPQRSTUVWXYZABCD
HIJKLMNOPQRSTUVWXYZABCDEFG
MNOPQRSTUVWXYZABCDEFGHIJKL
UVWXYZABCDEFGHIJKLMNOPQRST

"So, let's apply the key of the correct alphabet and see if it gives us anything . . ."

John paced, as my mom, Danny, Olive, and Mr. Bennett sat on the sofa, watching. John stopped behind my chair and put his hands on my shoulders, offering a supportive rub. No one seemed to notice or care but me. He couldn't stand being in the dark anymore. "Please, Digit, explain it to me."

"Sure." I slid the paper with the letters in the Caesar-shifted grid so he could see them. "I'm hoping that if I place the alphabet in its correct order above my grid and use it as a key, I can decode this by finding the code letter in each row and then marking the corresponding letter in the key above."

"I have no clue what you're talking about." You could really love a guy who was that honest.

"Try it," I said. "The first two rows were identical to the key so 'M' is 'M' and 'O' is 'O.' But in the third row, if you find the 'D' and go straight up to the key it's really 'C.' Go to the fourth row and find the 'M' and go straight up, you get to 'K' and so on.

Key: ABCDEFGHIJKLMNOPQRSTUVWXYZ
　　　ABCDEFGHIJKLMNOPQRSTUVWXYZ M → M
　　　ABCDEFGHIJKLMNOPQRSTUVWXYZ O → O
　　　BCDEFGHIJKLMNOPQRSTUVWXYZA D → C
　　　CDEFGHIJKLMNOPQRSTUVWXYZAB M → K
　　　EFGHIJKLMNOPQRSTUVWXYZABCD I → E
　　　HIJKLMNOPQRSTUVWXYZABCDEFG Y → R
　　　MNOPQRSTUVWXYZABCDEFGHIJKL K → Y
　　　UVWXYZABCDEFGHIJKLMNOPQRST I → O

John stared over my shoulder as I worked through the grid. The answer was MOCKERYO. John was confused. "So that's the attack site? Mockeryo? What's that?"

"I'm not done. There are fifteen more letters in the code, FDBTAQZMDIBIVHY, so we have to repeat the grid twice." I copied it again.

Key: ABCDEFGHIJKLMNOPQRSTUVWXYZ
　　　ABCDEFGHIJKLMNOPQRSTUVWXYZ F → F
　　　ABCDEFGHIJKLMNOPQRSTUVWXYZ D → D
　　　BCDEFGHIJKLMNOPQRSTUVWXYZA B → A
　　　CDEFGHIJKLMNOPQRSTUVWXYZAB T → R
　　　EFGHIJKLMNOPQRSTUVWXYZABCD A → W
　　　HIJKLMNOPQRSTUVWXYZABCDEFG P → I
　　　MNOPQRSTUVWXYZABCDEFGHIJKL Z → N
　　　UVWXYZABCDEFGHIJKLMNOPQRST M → S

Key: ABCDEFGHIJKLMNOPQRSTUVWXYZ
　　ABCDEFGHIJKLMNOPQRSTUVWXYZ D → D
　　ABCDEFGHIJKLMNOPQRSTUVWXYZ I → I
　　BCDEFGHIJKLMNOPQRSTUVWXYZA B → A
　　CDEFGHIJKLMNOPQRSTUVWXYZAB I → G
　　EFGHIJKLMNOPQRSTUVWXYZABCD V → R
　　HIJKLMNOPQRSTUVWXYZABCDEFG H → A
　　MNOPQRSTUVWXYZABCDEFGHIJKL Y → M

"MOCKERYOFDARWINSDIAGRAM," I read. "Mockery of Darwin's Diagram."

My dad had been watching me work from across the table, reading upside down so he was a little behind. "What does that mean? Is it something about natural selection?"

When I looked up, I had tears in my eyes. "I have no idea. We're almost out of time. We're not going to make it." I'd used up a lifetime of mental energy decoding their string of letters and now this? Darwin? I knew next to nothing about Darwin.

John was pacing behind me, making me anything but relaxed. "Mr. Higgins? Does it mean anything to you? Where would we find a Darwin diagram?"

My dad was studying the decoded message when Olive popped off the couch, raising her right arm, like she was desperate to be called on to be the snack helper. "I know this!" She came over to the table, dangerously close to being within smacking distance.

"Olive, seriously, this is really important." I was pleased with my restraint.

"No, really." Hair flip over the shoulder. "I am in the Biology Club, you know."

"Still?" I'd thought that was a one-semester boo-boo.

"Yeah. And last fall we did a whole month called 'Digging on Darwin.' We all read *On the Origin of Species* and did a project on it. We made a Tree of Life out of the lids of my old shoeboxes. It was in the front hall of our school for a whole semester. Farrah, where have you been? It's like you don't even know me."

Is it possible to be so busy thinking people are stupid that you forget to notice that they're not? Is it possible that we were having this conversation when there were forty minutes to stop a bombing? "I'm sorry, Olive. Go on."

"So the display we made was exactly like the diagram in Darwin's paper. It's the only diagram in the whole thing, and he uses it to describe how all of life is connected. The Tree of Life has 'ever branching and beautiful ramifications.' That's a quote." She raised both of her eyebrows at me for emphasis. *I'm sorry, who are you, and what have you done with my blond friend?*

My dad had no problem taking help from Olive. "That's exactly what it is. The Tree of Life. Where would there be a mockery of it?"

Olive was on it again, arm raised and waving. "I think I know that too. When we were designing the project, I researched other drawings and sculptures of the Tree of Life. The coolest one was at the Animal Kingdom at Disney World. But I didn't have enough shoeboxes to pull it off. Hard to believe, right? Anyway, it's this huge concrete and plastic tree that's supposed to have a representation of every animal in the world. Like a fake tree would be a mockery, wouldn't it?"

I made a mental note to look into the existence of parallel universes, because I was pretty sure I'd slipped into one. My dad was nodding at her. "That has to be it. Imagine how Jonas Furnis would regard a plastic tree that purports to be a symbol of the connectedness of the natural world."

That was enough for Mr. Bennett. "We'll have to have to send a squad to Disney World immediately. But we'll work through the CIA. We cannot risk tipping off the FBI in case Steven had an accomplice there."

He got on the phone and in a slow and measured voice described only the most pertinent details: There was good reason to believe that Jonas Furnis was planning to attack Disney World in the next thirty minutes, and there was no time to explain. A full debriefing would follow after the crisis was averted.

This was background noise. I got up from the table and hugged Olive. "I don't know who I thought you were."

"Uh, same here? And why is everybody calling you Digit?"

"Danny can explain it to you. And, Danny? My kid brother? Really? What's with you two?"

"He's an awesome guy."

I couldn't argue with that. I curled up in my mom's arms on the couch, physically and emotionally wiped out. Maybe I was a little out of shape. I closed my eyes and prayed that we were right and that they could be stopped in time and captured and that this would be over. At some point my mom got up and John took her place, holding me and stroking my hair. I guessed the cat was out of the bag about us, and it seemed not to matter, anyway. I snuggled up to his chest, feeling like I never wanted to move again.

I didn't lift my head or open my eyes until I heard Mr. Bennett answer a call and say, "Got 'em? How many? Great? Uh-huh. Okay, great work, that was close. Tell Jameson I'll call him in a few hours and give him the whole story. In the meantime, I need an unmarked car and a body bag at the following address . . ."

"Hey, Digit." John was holding me tight. "It's okay. It's over. You did it. They're safe." Relief poured over me. I wiped my eyes.

Steven's body was carried out by two plainclothes CIA agents and tossed into the back of a Chevy Suburban. My mom busied herself in the kitchen, searching for appropriate post-terrorist-catching snacks. Seemed like an occasion for a nice Chex Mix.

Danny came over and kissed the top of my head. "Nice work, Digit." He and Olive looked a little freaked out and went up to his room, presumably to process what they'd just seen.

"I want that bikini back . . ." I called after them.

My dad sat in his favorite chair, still and silent, watching John and me curiously. I felt like with all we'd seen in that room today, coming clean about a little romance wouldn't be such a big deal. I decided to open the lines of communication.

"What?" I asked.

"Nothing," he said, with smiling eyes and a little nod. "It's okay. I think it's okay."

"Thanks," John said, understanding the meaning of the moment much sooner than I did.

Mr. Bennett rushed into the room, phone in hand but away from his ear for the first time in an hour. "John, we've got to get going. We have two senior CIA agents and a representative from the Homeland Security office meeting us at the FBI in fifteen minutes. We'll retrieve Steven's file on Jonas Furnis and then meet with Damage Control."

"Damage Control?" I asked. "For what?"

"A media-savvy team is meeting already to figure out how to unwind this whole lie. We need to get you unkidnapped and into your normal life but keep it out of the press so that Jonas Furnis will continue thinking you are dead until they are shut down and have bigger problems. When they find out we have all their financial records and hopefully taped correspondence, they're not going to worry about one girl who can identify one operative." Mr. Bennett was already walking out of the room as he finished his sentence. "John, come on!"

John got up and started to follow his dad out, as if by habit. He stopped and turned back around to me and took my hand. "I'll come back later."

"Okay." I didn't get up. Was he really leaving?

He walked over to my dad, who stood, and shook his hand. "Thank you for everything, Mr. Higgins. I'm really glad we could bring her back safely." He blushed a little at his understatement. He started to say something else to my dad but changed his mind. Then he turned to me and started to say something and again changed his mind. Finally he turned and left.

My dad came over and sat by me, a little smug. "So, you're in love. It's about time."

I shoved him a little. "He said he was coming back, right? I heard him say that—did you?"

"Yes, sweetheart, but probably not tonight. He lives here, doesn't he? He will probably take his dad back to his apartment and come back in the morning. Are you hungry?"

"No, I'm going to bed." I walked up to my room and did a nosedive into my bed. I imagined I could still smell John there, feel his imprint from the night before. But I really couldn't. That annoyed me. In the movies, people are always sniffing stuff to catch a whiff of their absent lover. In real life, things just smell like Bounce dryer sheets.

I got in bed, my own bed, for the first time in what felt like months. I stared up at my bumper stickers, all so familiar but new somehow. Everything was new, but it was as if hunting terrorists, cheating death, and falling in love had changed my very DNA. And now all that was nearly over, except for the John part. That was just starting. Right?

I sat up in bed. *What now?* I wondered it for the first time. Life had been so minute to minute, everything changing on a dime, and I hadn't really thought through to next week and next month. This thing between John and me wasn't going to be like a wartime romance, over when life was back to normal, was it? I mean, I was probably going back to school on Monday. He was going to go back to managing the Fruitcake Room. Would I see him at night? Talk on the phone? Then it would be summer and I'd have lots of time, but he had a job. We could figure it out, I guess. The thought of spending this whole night without him was excruciating, and the idea that I'd be at school all day with him working nine to five was more than I could consider.

But then I was moving to Boston at the end of August, starting college, and going in a totally different direction. Would we do that long-distance relationship thing that never works out on TV? Maybe by August we'd be on sounder footing, and our relationship could stand the distance. The truth was that I really had no idea what tomorrow was going to look like. I just knew that tomorrow I would wake up and think about John before I thought about anything else. I knew that I loved him and felt like he loved me too. That would be enough, right?

MAY YOU LIVE IN INTERESTING TIMES

I WAS UP AND FULLY DRESSED by seven. I still couldn't leave the house and had no idea how to get in touch with John. When the phone rang at eight, I sprinted to the kitchen to see my dad already had it. "Sure, John, she's right here."

I nearly ripped the phone from his hand, trying to calm my stomach and my voice before I said anything. Did I really think he was just gone? I took a few steps out of the room before speaking. "Hey."

"Hey. You know this is the first time I've ever spoken to you on the phone? Am I calling too early?"

"No, this is great, I've been up forever." I plopped down on the couch, hoping this call would last for hours.

"I didn't sleep either. I guess I've gotten used to you." He was so normal, he could have been sitting right next to me. This was going to be okay.

"Are you coming over?" I asked, relieved that we weren't going to be playing it cool.

"Actually, I'm calling to give you guys the official schedule of the day. Can your parents bring you to FBI headquarters at ten? You'll have to lie down in the back, so as not to be seen. Damage Control wants to go over some things with you, and I think the Bureau chief is going to come in with a team to debrief us. No big deal, but they are going to ask a ton of questions about what happened, for the record, before we totally forget."

"Sure, we'll meet you there," I said.

"Okay, good."

"Okay." A few seconds passed.

"And then, I was going to ask you, um, my dad is flying back to New York tonight, and I was wondering if you'd want to . . . I mean, if your parents would let you come hang out here tonight. I'd pick you up and bring you home at whatever time they said. We could just hang out like regular people, order a pizza, and watch a movie." Was he actually nervous to ask me that?

"It's a date. I can't think of anything in the world I'd rather do." This whole being-straight-with-people thing was getting to be a habit.

"Me either. It was all I could think about last night, just imagining what it would be like to have you here. Farrah, this is all really strange for me. I've never felt like this before."

More with the honesty. "Neither have I, not even close."

"I wish I knew how to make this day go by faster. Hang on." John put his hand half over the phone and was talking to his dad. "Yes, I have her on the line. They are going to meet us at headquarters for the debriefing. Yes, I told her she should lie down in the back . . . Okay. Sorry about that Farrah. Let's just talk more about that at our meeting later."

I giggled a little. "Okay. See you at ten." That was only in two hours, I told myself. I could make it.

My parents and I arrived at FBI headquarters a little before ten. I gave a wave to the surveillance cameras, knowing the security guys would recognize me and have a chuckle. In the lobby, we were escorted to an elevator bank that took us to the thirty-ninth floor. John was standing there, waiting in another expensive gray suit, when the doors opened. I tried as hard as I could not to throw my arms around him, managing to stop at a little pat on the arm. "Hi."

"Hi, Farrah. Mr. and Mrs. Higgins, please come this way. Damage Control is waiting in the conference room." John was a little stiff, but I overlooked it since he was at work. We'd snuggle up later.

We were greeted by a Damage Control committee of six who informed us, moment by moment, how the next twenty-four hours would go. Thursday morning a police car would arrive at our house, tipping off the neighbors that something was happening. My parents would call friends and family, telling them that I had escaped unharmed and had found my way to the police, who had brought me home. I would resume my normal life and be back at school on Monday, saying, "I'd rather not talk about it," when asked about my captivity.

John gave me a wink, and my stomach did a flip. My dad asked, "Won't the press be all over us? When they find out that she's been released, it'll be all over the news. How will you protect Farrah until Jonas Furnis is shut down?"

"Homeland Security," began the head Damage guy in a slow, deep voice, "has contacts in every major television and radio station. They can quiet any story they want for several weeks if it is in the interest of national security. The only discussion of Farrah's return will be among local gossips until we give the press the go-ahead. And by then no one will care. We do this all the time."

We nodded, as if we were satisfied by their plan and as if we had a choice. I looked at my watch to see that only thirty minutes had passed. How long till pizza and movies?

Just then the conference room door opened, and I noticed everyone sucked in a little air. A large man in a dark suit filled the door frame with eight people behind him. He looked more like a Wall Street type than an FBI guy and commanded such complete attention over the room that I wondered if he had bacon in his pocket. No one moved until John stood up and walked over.

John spoke with an outstretched hand. "Hello, sir, welcome. We are just finishing up with Damage Control here, and I think that the Higginses are adequately prepared for the next steps. Please come in. Mr. and Mrs. Higgins, I'd like you to meet our FBI Bureau chief, Don Woods. And this is Farrah Higgins . . ."

We all stood up and shook hands. Don looked me up and down and said without humor, "You seem to have survived well. I am glad."

On cue, all the Damage Control people stood up and backed out of the room, saying goodbyes and freeing chairs for the next group. Don Woods and his people sat down opposite us at the table, hands folded. I took the first seat closest to the door, and John carefully led my parents to the seats next to me, separating me from him and his dad.

The man to the far left spoke first. "We have prepared our preliminary questioning about the events of the last week: the initial contact with Jonas Furnis, Steven Bonning's duplicity, the financial records you obtained, your whereabouts in New York, your return here, the involvement of Henry Bennett, and finally the intelligence surrounding the events at Disney World. Please give short answers."

And so it began. They fired questions at us, mostly at John and me, but some at Mr. Bennett. We gave answers like: "On day three, in the Lost and Found," "PS 142," "West Side Highway." And the whole story came out. At one point I was asked to decode MODMIYKIFDBTAPZMDIBIVHY using the Fibonacci sequence and the Caesar shifts. At noon they brought in sandwiches, lemonade, and iced tea, and we kept on answering questions.

Finally at two p.m., there was nothing else to say. The man at the far left of the table said to the tape recorder, "This satisfactorily concludes the questioning of John Bennett, Farrah Higgins, and Henry Bennett in the likely capture of Jonas Furnis."

Don Woods finally spoke. "This concludes your involvement in this investigation. The CIA will be handling Jonas Furnis and Steven Bonning's role there for obvious reasons. The last item of business is what to do about you, John. After you have secured the safety of this young woman, unearthed a spy among us, and all but ensured the eradication of one of the world's fastest-growing terror organizations, I cannot exactly send you back to work receiving tips from the public."

Laughter all around. John's dad seemed really proud, and John smiled humbly.

"So I have spoken with the folks in D.C.," he went on, "who have been seeking to fill an opening in Special Sector, and I have recommended you for the job. Their training schedule is tight, so if you accept the job, your flight leaves immediately."

John let out an audible gasp. "Sir, that is an honor. Thank you very much."

Mr. Bennett, the wisest person in the room, looked over at me. I met his gaze. *What about me?* my eyes shouted.

"Do you accept?" Don Woods asked.

John looked at his hands for an answer. "Of course—I'm ready to go now."

"Great. Ribowitz will get you outfitted and shipped out." He gave Mr. Bennett a little smile. "Whereabouts unknown. You know the drill."

John turned to his dad and hugged him. "Are you sure you know what you're doing?" Mr. Bennett asked.

"No. But it's all I've ever wanted."

"All?" his dad asked.

"Bye, Dad. I'll call when I can." Then, as if to end the conversation, he turned to my parents. "Mr. and Mrs. Higgins, it was so nice to meet you both. I'm sorry that you had to suffer through your daughter's absence. I'm so glad that she is home safely." *Wait. What?!*

I was the only person between him and the door, where Don Woods and his new life were waiting. I felt a shadow of my former self starting to speak to save face. "Hey, congratulations. I totally get it—thanks for everything." But she didn't speak, because she barely existed anymore. I was done saying things that weren't true and then hiding behind them. It was too late for that. I wasn't going to backtrack and pretend this didn't happen. It occurred to me to start crying, but why? I was slightly, just slightly, above tricking him into staying. All I could get out was, "No pizza?"

He barely looked at me, knowing that if any intimacy passed between us, his credibility with the almighty Don Woods would be gone. "I have to go. I really have to."

"You don't have to."

Our eyes met for a second before he brushed past me and out the door. I've heard people say that you can actually hear your heart break. I'm not sure if I did, but I know that I felt it. It was a bit like having an elephant kick you in the chest, knocking all the wind out of your lungs. In fact, my chest felt so heavy that I wondered if I was having a heart attack. My breaths were short and incapable of filling my lungs. I backed into the chair behind me and let my head fall into my hands, wondering how I was going to get out of that building.

Mr. Bennett's voice faded into a low rumble as he spoke to the lady who was waiting to escort us out. "If you wouldn't mind, may we please have a few minutes alone? I can show us all out."

She left without a word — seemed to be going around. My mom spoke first. "Oh, darling. How awful." She turned to Mr. Bennett. "What was so important about that job? Why would he just leave without giving it a second thought?"

My dad's face had gone gray. I could tell that he was actually feeling my pain. Is it even worth it to be that close to someone that you have to feel their pain too?

Mr. Bennett answered, "It's a long story. That job carried with it a bit of folklore in our family — it's like the one that got away. Farrah, I'm so sorry. I knew he wasn't listening to me. All I can tell you is that he's an idiot and a coward. Not all the time, but right now he is. He'll figure it out, and it will be too late. By then you'll be over this."

"I'll never be over this." I couldn't bear to lift my head and see them all watching me fall apart.

Mr. Bennett touched my chin and raised my face to meet his. "Listen, Farrah. I've never seen him like that with anyone, bringing you to our home, sharing himself, hanging on your every word. It was real, Farrah. He just blew it. I'm so sorry."

"Thank you. I need to go home now." They all nodded and gathered their things and escorted me to the door like I was made of sand and was about to slip through their fingers. How right they were.

I'M ONE BAD RELATIONSHIP AWAY
FROM OWNING 30 CATS

IT'S AN INTERESTING THING, GETTING DUMPED. I'd never had a boyfriend before, and I still wasn't totally sure that I had, but I knew that I loved someone and that he'd walked away. So by anyone's definition, I guess I'd been dumped. In this particular situation, your only choices are to suck it up and move on or to "go there." For those first couple of days, I went there. I got home from the FBI that day, put on my pajamas, got a pint of Chunky Monkey, and watched *The Notebook*. Five times. Everyone left me alone. I suspect they were a little afraid of me. I went up to my room and listened to Taylor Swift's "White Horse" on replay, knowing she was the only person in the world who could relate. My nerve endings seemed to be on the outermost parts of my body, ready for any stimulus to pass by and hurt them, inviting it, even. I knew what it meant to have your heart broken wide open, because I was roadkill.

Olive took Danny to the Senior Prom on Saturday night. I came down to the living room in my sweats to watch them take pictures. He wore a white tux that she'd picked out; she wore black. I watched them hold hands as they walked out, somehow happy for them and sick to my stomach at the same time. The limo pulled up in front of our house. Kat popped out of the sunroof with her arms in the air, dancing to the beat of music that I couldn't hear. I tried to imagine myself at the prom, if none of this had happened. Maybe with Drew, dabbing Scotch behind my ears to keep up appearances. I felt sorry for that girl, maybe more sorry than I felt for my new self. I went inside and popped in *The Notebook*. Again.

My mother woke me up Monday morning with a tray of ice-cold cucumber slices. "You're putting me on a diet?" I asked, rubbing my swollen eyes.

"Darling, you've been crying for five days—you look like a prizefighter. Let's just put these on your eyes to bring down the swelling before school starts." I wanted to tell her that I didn't really care that my eyes were swollen, but I found that I didn't even care enough to say that. I just lay back and let her tend to me.

An hour later I was seated behind the wheel of my trusty old Volvo wagon, headed to school. Getting dressed and getting into that car felt like moving through Jell-O, but I insisted on driving myself. It's weird enough appearing back at school, unexpected after a brief kidnapping, but I didn't need an entourage. My parents followed Danny and me to the car: "What are you going to tell people?"

"It doesn't matter. They can think what they want." And I rolled up the window against the cheery spring morning. I pulled out of the driveway and headed out, feeling Danny watching me.

I glanced over at him. "What are you staring at?"

"You're just so different. It's cool."

"Why? Because I got my heart broken? Yeah, cool."

"Sort of. I mean more because you're opened up. It's like my karate teacher says—you are more alive when you are feeling pain than when you are so careful that you feel nothing. Maybe after some time goes by, this will have been really great for you."

"You've got to be kidding me." I had the strangest desire to reach over, open his door, and kick him into traffic.

"I know Dad said we can't talk about him, but I liked the way you were when he was around. You were Digit again, like

172

when we were little. And if you can stay there, then, yeah, I think this was worth it."

"Danny, I really don't want to start crying again. Can we just stop talking?"

"Suit yourself." He turned up the radio and left me alone.

I have to say that depression or grief or shock or whatever can make you a bit of a badass. I parked my car and strolled with my little brother past all the people I'd turned to for approval all those years. Some followed me and asked a thousand questions; others stood back and whispered too loudly: "She looks different—think she was raped?" Danny turned to say something, but I grabbed his arm and led him inside.

In the hall, nothing had changed. My locker still opened with the same 19-9-24. All of my books were still inside with my rotting lunch from exactly nineteen days ago. Danny stood behind me, as if on guard, as I got my things for class. When I turned around, the Fab Four and Drew Bailey were all gathered behind him. The girls hugged me tentatively, Olive pretending like she was surprised I was back.

"Oh my God, Farrah, are you okay?" Kat looked legitimately worried.

"I'm fine. It wasn't that big of a deal." I know that my face told them otherwise. I imagined that I looked cracked, like a piece of china that had been dropped and had a web of lines running through it, threatening its structure from the inside out.

"Where did they take you?" Tish asked.

"Did you see us on TV?" Veronica was trying to hide her excitement.

"Yeah, you looked great." I looked for a hole in the circle they'd formed around me, but they were shoulder to shoulder.

Drew looked really concerned. "You guys leave her alone. I mean, I've heard that in these kidnappings they take you back to their ship and take out all your organs and do medical experiments."

I almost smiled, partly because that was so stupid and

partly because he'd nailed it—that was exactly how I felt. "I think that's in alien abductions. I'll see you guys later. I have to get to class."

Danny led me by the arm out of their circle, and we made our way through the sea of staring faces in the hall. I didn't care. I was even shocked that I ever cared. It was all so clear now that this person that they were gossiping about didn't really even exist. They had no idea who I was. And Danny was right—just because I was completely broken, I didn't have to go back there. I was probably incapable of it, and that was the only thing in the world that felt close to good.

That first day of school lasted forever. I had lunch in my math teacher's room, assuring her that I was fine and blowing through some tests that I'd missed. I was grateful that they were making me finish all the work I'd missed. And then I'd have AP exams and finals to kill the next few weeks. My mind seemed to offer a break for my heart. Letting my mind do that computing thing kept me afloat. It was so natural and so involuntary, it seemed to happen without me. Anything that required any effort at all, however, eventually required me to use my will. And my will to do things was gone.

In the weeks that followed, things were really different between me and the Fab Four. First of all, I found that there was nothing I could do to get them to dump me. I told them I wasn't really interested in drinking as a sport. I told them I wanted to stay home Friday night to watch *Cosmos* on PBS. I told them my SAT scores. I told them about MIT. I was completely in their face with Digit, and they were unfettered. I wondered if they'd been true friends all along. Or if my cachet as Party Girl was nothing compared to my status as Kidnapping Victim. I'd gotten them on TV, for God's sake.

The second change was me. I saw them now from the perspective of someone who had watched Olive save the lives of hundreds of people through her knowledge of science. What else was possible? Kat's sarcastic comments suddenly had humor to them. Veronica was still no genius, but she seemed softer and sweet. I found out that Tish took classes at the Santa Monica Arts Center and was really into sculpting. Where had I been?

My days were busy with normal stuff like school and homework. But when that wasn't enough to fill the time, I found myself diving into the less healthy side of Digit. I made a habit of taking everything out of the linen closet—and I mean everything: flat sheets, fitted sheets, hand towels, bath towels—and ironing them into perfect nine-inch squares. The shelves in the closet were thirty-two inches wide, so I was able to place three stacks on each shelf, perfectly equidistant, with one and one-quarter inches separating them from each other and the walls. Temporary relief.

My nights were brutal. I alternated between staring at the ceiling and staring out my window, torturing myself by replaying every moment: the days in the warehouse, laughing at Luke and Scarlet, the flight to New York, the cramped secret townhouse entrance, the first kiss, the one and only phone conversation, the end. I wanted to tell myself that it didn't make sense, that it'd been a mistake, and that he'd be back. But I was fully committed to being honest, even with myself. I had known he had a tendency to shut down and go robot. Even his dad had seen this coming and had tried to warn me. If all of his girlfriends had told him he was emotionally unavailable, why was I going to be any different? Could someone get me Oprah's number?

On the one-month anniversary of my broken heart, I had a little knock on my door at around two a.m. Danny walked in, rubbing his eyes, and sat down on the side of my bed. "Man, Digit, you were hit pretty hard. Think you'll ever sleep again? I can hear you in here every night, in bed, out of bed, in the bathroom, back in bed. It's exhausting."

I smiled at his concern. "I don't know. I've never seen this movie before. Is it going to be a week and I'll wake up okay, or will it be a lifetime of regret and a house full of cats? I have no idea."

"I liked him. I don't now, of course, don't get me wrong. But I thought he was cool and sort of genuine, in an old dude sort of way."

"I guess he was, until he wasn't."

"I don't get that, Dig. But what I know is that you are a cool girl. I've thought you were cool ever since you put my Hot Wheels Volcano together on Christmas Day when no one else wanted to. I mean, you saved all those people at Disney World, all those kids. I don't think you really see how important you are, and I don't just mean since that guy dumped you. I mean ever."

I didn't know what to say to that. He was painting a picture of me that was so far from the victim I felt like.

"Don't get me wrong—I wouldn't want to be like you. It makes me tired just thinking about it. But it's like you observe the world from a slightly different angle than everyone else. And it makes you really powerful. I guess I just wish you could find a way to let that make you happy."

"Jeez, Danny. That's deep. Where are you getting all this?"

"It's the ka-ra-te. Powerful stuff, Digit. Powerful stuff."

I laughed and gave him a hug. I'd envied that kid for so long—it was like he was born at Disneyland with a FAST-PASS in his hand. It made me feel good that he admired me and all the crazy things that made me different. We could probably learn a lot from each other. He left and shut the door. I saw the bumper sticker that read GOD BLESS THE WHOLE WORLD. NO EXCEPTIONS. Nice.

After a few weeks, I asked my dad if I could come to UCLA after school. He had never let me before, saying I needed to do normal kid things while I could. Now he realized that normal was not an option, that I wasn't going to come home and announce that I'd joined the cheerleading squad. He seemed happy that there was something I wanted to do, anything, so he agreed. He put me in a "Nonlinear Dynamics and Chaos" seminar and let me work on the assignments and take the tests. It helped.

As I lay in my bed on night forty-three of my imprison-ment in hell, I realized that the fact that it was over wasn't the worst part. The worst part was that I had been so wrong. I had become my truest most authentic self; I had listened to my instincts and followed them completely. I had opened up and jumped in . . . and I had been completely wrong. That was the piece that was going to take the longest to heal. I'm sure that replaying that week in my mind, dissecting it like it was a Faulkner novel, wasn't helping. Intellectually, I could go back and see where I might have been smarter to keep my guard up, where he was showing me that he wasn't going to stick around. But whenever I fell asleep, I was always remem-bering that feeling I had when I was within reaching distance of him, and I was baffled to think he hadn't felt it too.

LOVE YOUR MOTHER

A WEEK BEFORE GRADUATION, MY GRANDPARENTS (both sets) arrived from Seattle and Denver. Luckily, the news of my kidnapping had never made it out of state, so there was no dramatic reunion. My house was such a frenzy of activity that no one had any patience for my sulking. That was probably just what I needed. Six weeks had passed. I'd heard nothing from John and didn't even know where he was. It was over.

My parents planned a huge graduation party. I'm sure it was a lot more extravagant than it would have been if they hadn't been so worried about me. I woke up on the morning of my graduation to a house full of hot pink peonies. My mom had gone to the flower mart at five a.m. to get them and had arranged them in vases around the house and on small tables in the yard. I smiled when I saw them and then saw her watching me with tears in her eyes. She looked so tired.

"Mom, this is so beautiful. Are you okay? I'm not leaving until August . . ."

"I'm fine. It's just that I hadn't seen you smile in so long. I've just been so worried about you." She grabbed me and hugged me like I'd been away at war. And I guess I had.

"I'm going to be okay, and I'm sorry that you and Dad have had to go through all of this." I wiped a tear from her face. "But I hope you didn't want grandchildren because I guarantee I will never be involved with another man—I think they're all terrorists." She gave me a little smile. "I'm going to be okay."

We laughed and hugged a little and then walked around looking at all the party preparations. The doorbell rang, and I went to get it. "Jeez, Mom. More flowers?" I said as I came back into the kitchen. I was holding a small bouquet of baby roses in a square glass vase. They were all shades of white and the palest pink.

"I didn't order those," she said. And then our eyes met, and she grabbed the vase as I started to lose my grip. I couldn't move.

"Please open the card, Mom. I can't do it." My heart was pounding so fast that I had to steady myself against the kitchen counter.

"'Congratulations to a most outstanding girl. Henry Bennett.' Oh. That was thoughtful," she said.

Disappointment threatened to pull me under again. I knew he meant well, but it was sort of like pulling off a scab that had just started to heal. "It's just so sad, Mom. We really knew each other; it's not like it was just some mad crush. Everything about us together was so right, like we'd been waiting for each other or something. And to have him just leave without a thought makes me think I was crazy."

"You were not crazy, darling. I saw it too. I never saw you as at ease with another person. And the way he looked at you . . . Well, this isn't helping. But I cannot get onboard with Henry and call him an idiot and a coward, because I think he is neither. I think he cares about you a great deal, but I think he cares about his career more."

"Great." That wasn't exactly what I wanted to hear.

"I know a lot about people, Farrah. And I know that men that age can feel inadequate and fearful about their future. It's as if they have to get themselves to a certain place before they feel worthy of that big relationship. They don't understand that on their own they have enough to offer."

I nodded in agreement. "I know that's true. But his dad

did it—he risked his career to be with Mrs. Bennett, and it all worked out. And I mean, it's not like I wanted the guy to buy me a house and get me pregnant. I just wanted to watch a movie and eat pizza with him and see where it went."

"I get the feeling he's not a let's-see-where-it-goes kind of person. Which is too bad, because life's best experiences usually happen when you're making other plans." She walked over and put her arm around me. "You'll get through this. You're brilliant and seventeen, two of the best things you can be. Now let's get you into that putrid gown and get going."

THE TRULY EDUCATED NEVER GRADUATE

MY GRADUATION STARTED AT 11:30 ON what had to be the hottest day of the year. There were 790 kids sitting up on a stage melting in black polyester caps and gowns. Our principal spoke; we sang; our valedictorian spoke; we sang; some woman who had started with nothing and hit it big spoke; we sang. There were sixteen awards, and I won four. Thank God, because the only relief I got from the heat was the breeze up my gown when I walked across the stage to receive an award and shake hands with the principal. I was a little dizzy looking out into the crowd. My parents and all four grandparents were in the twenty-fourth row toward the aisle. I imagined my parents older and squinted to morph their parents' faces over theirs. This wasn't hard to do with the sweat dripping down into my eyes. I imagined that the guy standing behind the last row of chairs, who must have been sweltering in that suit, was John. That he'd helicoptered in from points unknown to be here today, to tell me he was an idiot and a coward. And that I'd been right about us.

Then I imagined he was looking right at me, raising his left hand in a little wave. Kids were passing wet washcloths around to cool us down. One came my way, and I wiped my face temporarily cool. I looked out again. I raised my hand slowly to give a low wave back, just to see if I was crazy. He waved again, and I saw a small sad smile. I was going to need some Gatorade and some professional help.

Mercifully, we processed off the makeshift graduation stage into the air-conditioned gym for cold drinks. I dumped my gown in the collection bin and went to find my family. My grandparents had had all they could take of the heat and went to meet us at the house. My parents congratulated me about a thousand times as I scanned the crowd for this ghost I'd imagined.

"Honey, are you okay?" My dad had his arm around me as he led me to the car.

"I'm fine, great. Just hot and maybe going a little crazy. Let's get going so we can beat our party guests home."

Danny said, "By the time we get home, Nana will have the house cooled down to about fifty-nine degrees. You'll be begging to be back in your toasty polyester gown." I paused for a minute in the parking lot, waiting to see a figure in a dark suit approach. The crowds broke up—moms, dads, little kids, old people fanning themselves. No prince. No white horse.

In the car, my mom read the inscriptions on all of my awards. My dad wondered aloud at how long it would take to get to the dorms at MIT from our front door, including getting in the car, driving to the airport, waiting in the security line, et cetera. Mom, Danny, and I waited patiently as he worked it out (eight hours, twenty-three minutes, just so you know), and assured himself that it wasn't really that far.

ACTIONS SPEAK LOUDER THAN BUMPER STICKERS

⟳

WE LAUGHED AS WE WALKED IN through the kitchen door and got hit by the ice-cold air. "Nana? Granny? Aren't you freezing?" I stopped as I got to the living room, frozen myself. He was seated on the smaller sofa, between my two grandmothers, smiling shyly. "Hi."

"Sweetheart, your friend came to the party a little early, so we are all just getting acquainted. We didn't know you had a friend who used to work for the FBI — how fabulous!" Did you guess that was my mom's mom?

"Used to?" I asked. My parents were standing behind me, I'm sure as shocked as I was. John freed himself from the grandmothers and walked toward me.

My dad stepped in front of me protectively.

"Sir, may I just speak to her for a minute? I've come a long way," John said.

"You'd better have." My dad moved out of the way, and there was John standing three inches from me. I scanned myself for feelings: angry, hurt, excited. They were all there. My heart was beating so fast that I had an instinct to run away, but instead I stood there staring.

"Digit, can we go outside for a second?" He had the nerve to take my hand, and I let him. We walked out the front door and took a seat on the steps. I could tell he was really nervous, so I thought I'd break the ice.

"Your dad thinks you're an idiot."

"I've heard. He wrote me a letter outlining all of my short-comings. It seems that this last move was the icing on the cake. He really thinks I blew it."

"I could have told you that."

"I'm really sorry." He waited for me to say something. Probably the something that part of me wanted to say: *It's okay. Let's go back to the way things were.* But it wasn't okay, so I said nothing. He went on, "I felt like I didn't have a choice."

"If that had been me, I would have felt like I didn't have any choice but to stay. I couldn't have left you like that."

"Then maybe you're a little quicker than I am." He was quiet for a while, studying my hand. "The minute I got on the plane, I knew I'd made a mistake. But I just kept thinking it would get better, that the ache I felt would go away. I told you I've never felt anything like this before; I didn't know how long it would last."

"It's not the stomach flu."

He laughed. "I know. I guess I was just testing it to see if it was real. I mean, I was with you for a week and a half, under the strangest of circumstances. Standing in front of my big career break, I wasn't sure."

Great. "So why are you here?"

"It didn't take me this long to figure out how I feel. I knew in the first twenty-four hours, but it took me this long to get out of the decision I'd made. The whole time we were apart, I had this anxious feeling like I'd left my car running. Like there was something I needed to get back to urgently." He took both of my hands now, so serious that I was going to overlook the stupid leaving-the-car-running analogy. "I knew that I loved you when we were in the warehouse, studying our transcripts. I knew it was something real, but I was sure it was wrong, given the circumstances. And when we were on the plane to New York and I was watching you sleep for three hours straight, I promised myself I wouldn't act on my feelings, not because I knew it would get me into trouble, but because I wanted to protect you more than anything in the world. And when I finally got to hold you all night in that middle school, I knew I was cheating, but I'd never gone to sleep so happy."

I still said nothing. I was hoping for more. I got:

"I went to the other side of the world to understand what this is. I love you. And it's not going to change. Ever."

My heart was racing. I wanted so much to jump into his lap, but I was still so raw. I continued my interrogation.

"So you quit?"

"I quit. I called Don Woods and told him the truth: I've fallen in love, and if I don't find out where this is going, I know I will regret it for the rest of my life. Well, I used my own words."

"You've fallen in love." I found it soothing to repeat the words. "What did he say?"

"I was surprised that he was so cool about it. He told me that at twenty-one, I owed myself a little time. He offered to bring me home and give me the summer off, then in September I'm joining the Terror Task Force in New York."

I didn't say anything. I just let him hold my hand and let it all sink in. He was back, he was in love, and he was staying all summer.

He went on. "I called my dad on the flight here. He wanted to know if I'd bothered to find out if you were still interested in me before I quit my job. Then he wanted to know if I'd bothered to send flowers. He concluded by telling me that you're too good for me, anyway."

"I really like that man." There are so few times in your life when you feel like you are holding all the cards. I have to admit that I was enjoying it immensely.

"It's a good job. Not as prestigious as Special Sector, but a lot better than managing the public. I'll have weekends off, if you want me to come to Boston, but no pressure. I don't want to start making a whole new set of five-year plans. I just want to spend time with you before you move in August. I mean, if it's okay, if you still feel the same way. I'm so sorry I ever left you."

That was really all I'd needed to hear. I threw my arms around his neck and kissed him like it was going to save my life. We had no place to go. I didn't care if the guests started arriving or if my grandparents were spying out the window — which was likely.

"Is that a yes?" he asked, finally.

"Sure." He kissed me again, holding both of my hands in his.

"Just as a short-term plan, I was wondering if you'd come with me to Hawaii for a few weeks. We have a little house on the beach in Maui, and we could just hang out. I know I owe you a pizza."

"Hawaii?" My head was spinning. I really wanted to say something but didn't want to break the spell.

"If it makes you feel better, we can pretend we are being chased."

I laughed. "Okay, you can be in charge of making sure the doors are locked." A moment passed between us, both of us realizing we'd be alone together. Of course, we'd spent a week practically in solitary confinement together, but this was different and we both knew it.

"Are you eighteen yet?"

"My birthday is on Tuesday."

"We'll leave on Tuesday."

"Okay." He kissed me again, and I realized that I could have sat on that step forever. I didn't need to go to Hawaii; I would have been happy to be back in that dusty warehouse. But Hawaii sounded nice too.

He stood up and offered me his hand. "Let's go back in and face all those old people. Are you going to tell them about our trip, or should I?"

"You've got a whole lot of sucking up to do before they'll let me go anywhere with you. Maybe we'll just get through this party and take it from there."

He hugged me again, and I took a second to rest my head on his shoulder. Happiness filled every cell in my body. I'd been right. I'd been right to be myself, I'd been right to open up, and I'd been right to think someone could love me for it.

When I opened my eyes, I saw it for the first time. Parked right in front of my house. It had to be John's car, a blue Jeep, top off. And on the back, posted for the world to see, one single bumper sticker: MY GIRLFRIEND'S SMARTER THAN YOUR HONOR STUDENT.

Well, probably.

ACKNOWLEDGMENTS

Thank you to Helen Breitweiser, agent and friend, for her hard work and sense of humor. And to Julia Richardson for her clear thinking and great insights, and for seeing how hot math can be.

Thank you to Elaine Kaman Tibbals for letting me sit in her tree.

Thank you to my dad, Charles Schwedes, for all those lessons in dimensional analysis. Who knew I was listening?

My most heartfelt thanks to my children: Dain for reading critically and enthusiastically, Tommy for believing it would happen, and Quinn for inventing Jonas Furnis.

And to Tom Monaghan, thanks for everything. And I mean *everything*.